The Island Gang Narratives

Malcolm R. Gibbs

AUP UK
Terrestrial And Universal
Publications

Published in the United Kingdom
TAUP UK
Sheerness
Kent

enquiries@taup.uk

In references to the Isle of Sheppey and within the time-
line of everything that happens all attempts have been made to
keep true to its history and changes in landscape; although
some variations were necessary for the story.

The name Jack probably originated in medieval times as
a form of the name John, but implying 'not quite as important as
John'.

Prologue

> **RAF WESTCOTT**
> **KEEP OUT**

"I ain't goin' in there Charlie. We'll get 'anged."

Like so many thousands of young children at that time, ten year old Charles (Charlie) Hall and his twin brother William (Billy) Hall had been moved away from London during the early part of 1940. Children were sent to areas of the country that were deemed to be safe so Charlie and Billy found themselves taken from their home in Bethnal Green to the County of Wiltshire. Both of them were rather scruffy and rough looking in appearance but their father's strict discipline had kept the boys on the straight and narrow so far. Billy being of a quiet and very nervous character still worried about any form of doing wrong, but Charlie being rather more adventurous pushed his luck to the limit more and more.

They found themselves billeted with Mr and Mrs Philpott in a large house on the outskirts of the tiny village of Westcott. Country life was completely alien to Charlie and Billy but they quickly adapted to the wide open spaces, the wonderful woodlands and the strange animals which previously they had only seen pictures of, in books. Mr and Mrs Philpott were very kind and the boys liked the middle aged couple very much. The Philpotts had never had a family of their own so were inexperienced in the art of looking after children. Charlie and Billy Hall took full advantage of the situation.

"Don't be such a Scaredy Cat Billy. We ain't gonna get 'anged. Murderers get 'anged, not kids."

"It's an Air Force Station, Charlie, RAF. You know we keep bein' told we ain't gotta go in these places."

"It ain't proper RAF for the war, Billy, cos they wouldn't send us to a place what could get bombed."

"But it's still RAF."

"Look, RAF has planes. Can you see any planes?"

1

"No, but…."

"Ave you seen any planes going in and out?"

"No, but…"

"No! cos it's derrick." Charlie felt proud to be able to show off and use the word 'derelict'. He correctly remembered the teacher's explanation but had not quite got the word itself right.

"What's derrick?"

"It means it ain't used and fallin' to bits. There ain't nobody here Billy. There ain't nuffing here."

Situated at the top of Westcott Heath, and cut into the edge of Darkling Woods, RAF Westcott did indeed seem to be derelict. Apart from a high, but old, wire fence which surrounded the entire Base, adorned here and there with the occasional 'Keep Out' sign, the whole area looked like a small unkempt woodland coppice. Within that coppice could be seen a building which appeared to be an old accommodation facility and one other structure, a Nissen hut which nature had discreetly camouflaged with saplings and thick shrubbery.

Over the centuries, legends and strange tales of mysterious happenings and disappearances had made Darkling Woods an area to be avoided by local inhabitants and visitors alike, which made it an ideal spot for the small Air Base. Quite what the Air Force did there no one knew because there were no aeroplanes nor was there any room for aeroplanes to either land or take off; indeed there seemed to be very little activity at all. RAF Westcott caused no problems for the local community and in return the local community caused no problems for RAF Westcott.

A narrow lane, almost a mile long, bordered by thick hawthorn hedging on both sides and having no passing places or turning areas served the purpose of allowing authorised vehicles and personnel access to the base. At the junction of this lane and Westcott Road a small white sign with black writing simply announced: 'Private. No Through Road'.

"There might be guards watching us or people in those buildings over there what can see us." Billy continued to express his fears.

"Look, there ain't no guards and no people. I'm tellin yer, Billy, this place is empty. Now come on, stop bein' such a Scaredy Cat."

Within minutes, they had pulled a small section of fencing

wire clear of the ground and crawled under. Keeping low they crept through the thinning trees and worked their way towards the hut. Scrambling under bushes they found a hole where the corrugated roof met brickwork and, both being small in stature, managed to squeeze into the building. As their eyes slowly adjusted to the darkness they realised, to their disappointment, that it was empty. They had hoped to find some items of military debris that might be collectable.

"Come on Charlie, let's go. The Mr and Mrs will be wonderin' where we are."

"Don't worry about them Billy. They won't do nuffing."

"But I don't like it in 'ere, I'm scared Charlie."

Now that their eyes were fully accustomed to the darkness they could see that there was actually something in the building, a very large tarpaulin draped across one end of the hut.

"Come on, let's 'ave a look." Charlie called over his shoulder as he disappeared behind it.

"What's there Charlie?" When no answer was forthcoming Billy very gingerly lifted a corner and peered behind it.

"Charlie," he called out to his brother again but still there was no answer.

"Charlie, where are you?" He slowly entered one side of the tarpaulin, quickly walked through behind it and out of the other side.

"Don't muck about Charlie, you're scarin' me now." He shouted, and then jumped as Charlie suddenly leapt out from behind the tarpaulin.

"Quick, come and look Billy. You won't believe what's behind ere."

"Stop tryin' to scare me, Charlie. I just looked round there and there ain't nuffing."

"Come on Scaredy Cat."

Charlie grabbed Billy's hand and pulled him behind the Tarpaulin.

RAF Wescott 16th August, 1943.

Lieutenant General James Hempstead, Air Commodore Arthur Theobald and Simon Eldridge sat at a large table with RAF Policeman Robert Jessop seated opposite them.

"Wasn't there anyone patrolling the perimeter fence?" Simon Eldridge asked.

"No sir."

"And why was that?"

Lieutenant General Hempstead answered that question for the policeman. "As you know, Simon, to avoid attracting too much attention we have always operated a low profile security plan."

"But has it turned out to be far too low for something as important as this?" asked the scientist in disbelief.

"It has worked very well." The Lieutenant General defended the plan.

"Worked well? Two ten year old boys were able to just walk straight in, unchallenged."

"No sir," Robert Jessop answered, now wanting to defend himself. "They did not just walk in; they broke in by lifting a small area of the perimeter fencing and crawling underneath."

Simon Eldridge still wasn't happy about the security arrangements. He turned to the Military Officers.

"I think we need to review how we secure this area and I have been working on an idea."

"May I remind you, gentlemen," Air Commodore Theobald cut in. "That discussions other than the current investigation are inappropriate at this moment. The three of us will get together afterwards and you can go over your concerns then, Simon. But for the moment we must focus on what has happened here and how we deal with it." He turned back to the policeman. "Tell us exactly what happened."

"Yes Sir." Jessop paused momentarily before continuing. "At 1925 hours on the evening of 14th August I noticed the dogs becoming agitated."

"Sorry, but were you the only person on guard." Simon Eldridge butted in.

"Me and the dogs, yes sir."

The scientist shook his head. "Carry on." He said despondently.

"I leashed one dog and picked up my rifle. As we left…"

"We?" The Air Commodore butted in.

"Myself and the dog, sir."

"Of course, sorry. Continue please."

4

"As we left the Security Room the dog became even more excited so I prepared for an intruder. Then I saw a boy over near the hut. He was shouting and screaming so I held the dog on close leash and approached him. He was in an awful state, sir, shaking and screaming that his brother had just been killed by an explosion inside the hut."

"Did you hear an explosion?" The Air Commodore continued the questioning.

"No, sir."

"Was there any indication that there had been an explosion?"

"No, sir."

"What about the hut, was it intact?"

"Yes, sir."

"No apparent damage to it?"

"No, sir."

"Did you enter the hut?"

"No, sir, I don't have the authority or the means to enter."

"And there was no sign of another boy?"

"No, sir."

"So what did you do?"

"The security instruction is that, in the event of an incident, Lieutenant General Hempstead must be informed immediately. Therefore, I needed to get back to the Security Room so that I could make that telephone call to him. But the boy would not come with me at first; he got it into his head that I was going to take him to be hanged. I managed to grab him and drag him to the room but he kept screaming for his brother. I had to lock the door so he couldn't run away and I managed to make my telephone call. At 2030 hours the Lieutenant General arrived."

"Thank you, you may leave us now." The Air Commodore dismissed Robert Jessop.

When the RAF Policeman had left, the three men relaxed. James Hempstead and Simon Eldridge lit up cigarettes while Arthur Theobald turned to his pipe.

"So James, I assume that after initially talking to Jessop the first thing you did was to check the hut?"

"Actually, no it wasn't. We had a very frightened young boy here, although Jessop had managed to calm him down a little. So after Jessop explained what had occurred and told me there wasn't any sign of an explosion I talked to the boy for a while. I managed to get him to tell me his name and where he and his brother lived. Their home was in London, Bethnal Green to be exact, but they had been evacuated and were billeted with a couple called Philpott here in Westcott.

"Eventually the lad calmed right down. I asked him if he was hungry and when he said that he was I suggested going to the Mess Room. There is a medical kit in the kitchen so when I prepared a drink and a sandwich I slipped a strong sedative into the drink. He was asleep within minutes so I laid him on one of the lounge chairs and covered him with a blanket.

"Then I went to check the condition of the hut and, as Jessop reported, the outside was indeed intact and showed no sign of an explosion. I entered the hut and inside, as with the outside, everything was exactly as it should be. There definitely had not been an explosion of any size or form. I secured the hut and returned to Security. Once I knew the situation was under control I went off to see Mr and Mrs Philpott."

"How did they respond?"

"Absolute panic but eventually I managed to assure them that nothing had occurred for which they would be held responsible. I told them that Billy was safe and would be cared for in hospital until well enough to be reunited with his mother."

"Did you mention the explosion or tell them that one of the boys was missing?"

"No, I didn't mention an explosion but of course I did have to tell them that one of the boys was missing. I used the pretext that Charlie, the missing boy, had disappeared which tied in nicely with all those mysterious tales and then added that initial enquiries pointed to the possibility of him being abducted. This is the story I have stuck with and it seems to have been accepted by everyone, except Billy of course, but in time I hope he will come to accept it."

Air Commodore Theobald looked towards the Scientist. "So, Simon, you are now positive that the boy Charlie did go?"

"Yes."

"Is he alive and if so where is he?"

"On both counts, I'm afraid I don't know." was all Simon Eldridge could add.

Turning towards Lieutenant General Hempstead, "Do we have anyone looking for him?" the Air Commodore asked.

"As you know gentlemen everything is on hold at the moment but, yes, we are searching for him. Unfortunately it will be like looking for a needle in a haystack and in this case a bloody great big haystack."

"Well, no matter how big the haystack we must still keep trying to find that needle." The Air Commodore took a puff of his pipe. "Of course Billy Hall will have to be watched for the rest of his life to make sure that he doesn't ever do anything to compromise the Project."

"That has already been arranged.

Part One

The Beginning of the End

1

1999

Mike Samuels looked up from behind the very over crowded desk tucked into the corner of his second hand books shop 'Lost and Bound'.

"Hello Jack, long time no see, how you doing?"

"Same old, same old I suppose. Got anything new?"

"Has anyone ever told you that you are a miserable old sod Jack Duggan?"

"Yeh, many times; so have you got anything?"

"No, I don't think I have. What are you still looking for?"

"I've got all the Jennings books now. I'm still looking for a few more William stories but I can't seem to find many Biggles books at all."

"Well, like I said mate, I haven't got any at the moment. There's a big chest out back that has just come from a house clearance. You're welcome to sift through whatever's in there, Jack, but it's all rubbish as far as I can see. Anyway, go and have a rummage."

Jack passed through into the old, musty storeroom behind the book shop and looked into a tatty wooden tea chest. As he removed the books one by one he had to agree with Mike Samuels, they were indeed rubbish. But then he pulled out an old red hardback book, smaller than the others but in much better condition.

Checking the spine, "I don't believe it." Jack gasped, checking it again. "Number four." He delved further into the chest and pulled out five more of the same, once again he checked the spines. "The whole set one to six, wow." Jack Duggan turned towards the door.

"Bloody hell Mike, you didn't say you had these."

"What's that?"

"The Island Gang, and the whole set, all six of them."

Mike appeared in the storeroom.

"Who?"

"The Island Gang."

"Never heard of them, mate, who are they?"

"You are kidding me. I can't believe that you've never heard of Maurice, Michael, James, Penny and June. They called themselves The Island Gang and I used to love them as a kid. E W Whittall wrote stories about a group of children who meet up with each other every year whilst on holiday with their parents on the Isle of Sheppey. They had such wonderful adventures and I could relate to them because that's where I've lived, all my life."

Mike shrugged his shoulders. "Sorry no, they must have bypassed me. But take them Jack, you can have them."

Jack Duggan left the shop with six books and a smile on his face the like of which had not been seen for many years.

2

Forty five years of misery and misfortune was how Jack Duggan described his life. For him the glass was always half empty, never half full.

Misfortune that an accident as a child had left him with the slight limp that nobody else noticed, but to Jack it was one of the many things that he felt blighted his life.

Misfortune that when doing one of the dozens of nondescript jobs which he had undertaken in his life he had quit during the night shift and gone home to find his wife in bed with another man. He still did not accept how fortunate he had been when the ex-Mrs Duggan was institutionalised after violently killing her next husband with a kitchen knife.

Miserable that he loved books and really wanted to be an author or an award-winning journalist but no-one had ever given him the chance.

Miserable that although now working as a Freelance Journalist he still had not found the block busting story that would propel him into the big league. All he managed to achieve were a few short stories in one or two magazines and coverage of all the boring rubbish that the local newspaper deemed as news.

Unfortunately this dismal outlook on his life masked the one real talent he did have; the one talent that could have opened the way to so many opportunities for him. Jack Duggan had a gift when it came to history and historical dates. The discovery of that ability first came about during lessons at school when he quickly found that remembering Kings, Queens, Wars, Battles, World Events and all their relevant dates was just too easy for him. The young boy soon found that it amazed and amused people to try to beat him with their questions but every time he would reel off the relevant answers. He expanded his talent by reading everything he could find that involved dates and lists. During his school years he was the best friend of so many pupils who needed answers for their homework and a constant centre of entertainment to a whole host of other people who thought they could win.

But as teenage years and teenage ideals took over the next

stage of growing up he, like most teenagers of any era, was only interested in the 'now'. History became boring; his brain switched the gift off. In later years if he had just reconnected with that talent he could have done so much more but the depression about his life had already begun to drag Jack Duggan down. So, as for realising his dream and becoming an author; he just never found the inspiration.

The one joy that remained a constant in Jack Duggan's life was his collection of books written for children. As a child these books were where he had discovered his love for the written word but, like most people, adulthood brought about the disposal of childhood treasures. Since then, he had spent much of his time hunting through book shops, searching for copies of those books and had managed to replace many of the ones he loved.

Jack sat, feet up on the settee, with a cup of coffee on the floor beside him. At this moment in time he desperately needed a story and something had crossed his mind. Thumbing through the local newspaper he spoke out loud as if there was someone sitting with him. "I suppose I must have seen it many times over the years, but it wasn't until someone pointed it out to me last year that I took any notice and actually read what was written." Stopping at the Obituaries page he quickly scanned the notices. "And now here it is again this year. *In Memory of Wartime Evacuee Charles, (Charlie) Hall. Killed August 1943. Aged Ten Years. Always remembered. Ernie*"

3

Jack moved aside the name sign that read 'Miss Sylvia Stevens' and leaned over the desk.

"Come on Sly."

"Jack, I told you it's a no go."

Sylvia Stevens had worked for the 'Local' since… well; she would never say exactly how long she had been there. Only that she started in the office as a junior when she left school and had seen three name changes to the newspaper, two take overs and out lasted goodness knows how many editors. She was also Jack Duggan's best mate.

He stood up. "Sly, there's got to be a story here. I'll go and ask Mark. He's the editor; he must see that it has great possibilities."

"He may very well do, but he will also tell you no."

"I don't see what the big problem is."

"Since Phillip, that notice has been taboo."

"But the notice is still put in the 'Obits' every year."

"Yes, because it's placed by a paying customer. We can't be seen to censor or pick and choose who or what we print."

"So who's this Phillip then? What's he got to do with all of it?"

"Phillip Easterbrook."

"And he is?"

"Was."

"Ok. And he was?"

"Phillip was the best this paper ever had," she stopped and smiled when Jack frowned. "Yes, even better than you Jack Duggan. To tell the truth he was far too good for this little outfit. He could have done so much better for himself."

"Well if he was that good, what happened? What did he do?"

"Like you, he saw a story in the Memoriam Notice for wartime evacuee Charles Hall and went to interview Billy Hall."

"Billy Hall?"

"Come round here." and she tapped away on her keyboard as Jack moved round the desk. After a moment she turned the screen so he could see it better: *In Memory of Wartime Evacuee, Charles*

(Charlie) Hall. Killed August 1943. Aged Ten Years. Always remembered. Billy.

Jack looked at the screen then fished out the crumpled piece of paper from his pocket.

"Always remembered, Billy?" He turned to Sylvia. "This one says always remembered Ernie".

"All I know is that every single year since the end of the war this notice has been placed in our newspaper, and like I said, Phillip also saw a story and went to interview Mr Hall." She stopped.

Jack let out a big sigh. "And?"

"Jack, we've been friends for many years now, I don't want to see you come to any harm."

"Harm; is it that serious?"

"I don't know Jack. I really don't know."

"You know I love you to bits Sylvia Stevens, you're my best mate, but I'm a big boy now. I can look after myself."

"Can you Jack Duggan? Are you really sure about that?"

There was silence between them for a long while as they just looked at each other.

"I'll think about it Jack. Meet me tonight; you can treat me to dinner."

"You, Sylvia Stevens, are a darling."

"Don't get too excited. I only said I would think about it. If I decide no, then no it will be."

He kissed her on the cheek. "See you later."

"Remember lover boy," she called after him as he left the office. "If I decide no then it is no."

Once outside he searched his pockets for a scrap of paper and his pen. He needed to note down what Sylvia had told him already:

Notice every year - since war
Charles Hall - wartime evacuee - killed 1943
Originally Billy
Billy Hall?
Phillip Easterbrook – reporter
Something happened?
Notice now placed by Ernie

"In case the answer is no, I have a few snippets here to make a start for myself."

4

Sylvia Stevens was a strikingly beautiful woman. At the age of fifty six she still had the youthful appearance which ageing rich and famous women spent fortunes trying to regain. Even then, most of them did not come anywhere close to achieving what Sylvia Stevens had naturally.

Sylvia had never married and although there were several relationships during her life she had never truly loved any man, until Jack Duggan. Yet Jack and Sylvia's relationship had always remained purely on a 'best mates' basis. Even when there had been a whirlwind courtship and he announced that he intended to marry Suzanne Atkins she congratulated him and wished them both every happiness. Inside it broke her heart. The heartache became even worse when Jack and his wife moved away from the Island.

Suzanne Atkins had torn Jack apart and when he returned to Sheppey it took much care and support from his best mate to bring him back to the point where he seemed happy again. At least when they were together he was happy but she knew that when they were apart Jack Duggan was a completely different man; he would never be truly healed. At least Sylvia was going to give Jack every chance he needed.

At eight o'clock she entered their usual Restaurant; they hadn't needed to arrange where and what time. Jack sat there waiting for her and he looked up as she approached.

"Wow, Sylvia Stevens you look absolutely fantastic."

"Thank you Jack," she looked him up and down. "And you look - scruffy." Jack smiled. "That's better." She loved his smile.

Ordering their meals was automatic; on each visit they always chose the same items from the menu. Sylvia knew that this evening all Jack Duggan had on his mind was their conversation earlier in the day. Yes, she was going to tell him what she knew but first she wanted this to be an evening out like they always had; just the two of them and no talk about work.

"Jack." She took his hand across the table.

"Sly."

"Jack, I've decided to tell you about the notice and about

15

Phillip, although it's a bit of a mystery and there's not really much known about what happened," she paused as Jack squeezed her hand. "But let's enjoy the evening first. Afterwards we can go back to my place, or yours if you wish, then I'll go over what I know."

He lifted her hand and gently placed a kiss on it.

"Your place", he said.

In the comfort of her front room Sylvia instinctively poured Jack a double Jim Beam Bourbon Whisky over ice. She didn't have to ask what he wanted to drink; she knew.

"So come on Miss Stevens, tell me everything."

She gave him a long dark look. "Oh, thank you Sylvia for a lovely evening, I've really enjoyed it. And now this is really cosy, just the two of us together." She said sarcastically.

There was a startled silence, then Jack apologised. "Yes, sorry Sylvia. It has been a wonderful evening, as it always is when I'm with you."

She smiled at him. "Yes, it has and I'm sorry to sound grumpy but it's just that I'm worried about your interest in all this business surrounding Charlie Hall's memoriam." She paused and looked at him. "I know you're eager to hear all about it, Jack, but to be honest there's really very little to tell, so don't get your hopes up too high."

She topped up both of their drinks and snuggled up beside him on the settee.

"Every year since the end of the war Mr Hall placed the Memoriam Notice for Charles Hall, a Wartime Evacuee who was killed. Someone did once ask him why he placed it and at the time he just said that Charlie should not be forgotten.

"Several years ago when he heard about this, Phillip Easterbrook, sensed a story. He wondered why they both had the same surname and thought that possibly they were family or maybe even brothers. Being one who never wanted to miss out if there was ever the chance of a story he decided that he wanted to interview Mr Hall and arranged to go and see him.

"Every time I think about that telephone call, Jack, it always seems to have been a bit strange."

"How do you mean?"

"Well, maybe it's just me being silly but Phillip dialled the number from my office. I overheard him ask for Mr Billy Hall and then the person on the other end answered. I assume it was Billy Hall, because after a moment Phillip answered 'No Mr Hall my name is Phillip, Phillip Easterbrook'. He listened again and his face went a ghostly white. He stammered something like 'I need to see Billy urgently', and then added 'I can feel it. I remember now, I know what happened '. Phillip virtually fell out of the door in his haste to leave."

Momentarily she stopped and Jack didn't push her. He just cuddled her closer to him.

"Phillip was never seen again. He just disappeared."

"Where did he go?"

She looked up at him and frowned. "He disappeared, Jack. No one knows where he went."

"Yes, sorry." He thought for a moment. "So what did Mr Hall say about all this?"

"He had a heart attack that same evening and unfortunately died. Of course at the time we didn't actually know Phillip was missing, so no-one had a chance to ask him anything."

"A heart attack, that was a bit of a coincidence."

"Yes, I suppose it was."

"What about the police? Were they involved?

"Yes, but nothing."

"How do you mean nothing?"

"Exactly that, of course they thoroughly investigated events but discovered nothing at all."

"There were no clues or evidence as to what took place?"

"No."

Still cuddling her close Jack sat quietly. She looked up at him and spoke again.

"So you can see why no-one will have anything at all to do with that notice."

Jack was still puzzled. "So why is it signed Ernie, now?"

"The year after Billy Hall died the Notice didn't appear, but then a year on; the Memoriam was placed again."

"But this time it was by Ernie?"

"Yes."

"And no one knows who he is and why he now places the notice."

"No."

"Is he local?"

"I don't know, Jack, I don't know anything about him at all."

"Well, the first thing I need to do then is find out about this Ernie." He turned to look at the large decorative wall clock. "But for now, it's late Sly, look at the time."

She pulled herself in close to him, "Do you have to go?"

"I need to go home and get some beauty sleep. It's all right for you, you are beautiful enough already."

"Jack Duggan, you are a real smoothy."

At the front door she kissed him. Then, pulling him close to her, she kissed him again. Gently stroking a finger across his lips she purred.

"If I had my way, Jack Duggan, you would be crawling out of my bed in the morning, exhausted."

She didn't know what had made her say that. Maybe it was the drink, she didn't know.

They continued to hold each other "One day Sylvia Stevens, one day," and he gently kissed her. "Goodnight, Sly, sleep well."

"Good night Jack," she said, and then added. "Please be careful."

He remained on the step as she closed the door.

"Thank you, Sylvia Stevens, for a lovely evening and thank you for the information." That rare smile came to his face again. "And thank you for what you just said."

He set off on the twenty minute walk home, his mind going over what Sylvia had told him. At one point he stopped under a street light and stood thinking about all the things he had learnt during the day. He moved on and shortly afterwards stopped again. This time he found himself standing in the middle of the road but now his mind wasn't on the information Sylvia Stevens had given him; it was on what she had said as he was leaving.

The following morning Sylvia opened his front door with her spare key and went in.

"Jack." She called.

He came out of one of the doors and she ran down the corridor towards him.

"Sly, are you alright? What's the matter?"

She wrapped her arms round him.

"Nothing, it's just that I wanted to apologise for what I said last night." Although she didn't say exactly what she had said that made her feel the need to apologise, Jack knew and didn't embarrass her by asking. "I haven't slept all night, worrying in case I offended you."

"Well, Sylvia Stevens, you don't have to worry any longer because you didn't do or say anything to offend me." He winked at her and gave her a loving squeeze.

Sylvia smiled at him then stepped back and looked down. She had been so desperate to apologise that she hadn't noticed he was completely naked.

"For goodness sake Jack Duggan, go and get some clothes on. It's enough to put a girl off her breakfast."

"You make the coffee; I'll go and have a shower." He said as he turned away.

In the kitchen Sylvia removed the old filter and dregs from the machine and threw them into the bin. Then after fitting a new filter she added a large scoop of coffee and slid the filter drawer back in place. Finally, she poured a measure of cold water into the top of the machine. As the machine started to glug away, Sylvia leaned back against the work top. She could hear the shower running.

The bathroom door was slightly ajar and she gently pushed it a little further. Sylvia could now see him in the shower cubicle and watched as he soaped himself all over. Quietly she removed her clothes and slipped into the shower behind him...

"Is that coffee ready yet?"

Sylvia snapped out of her daydream as Jack entered the kitchen.

"Ready in a couple of minutes, the last drips are just filtering through."

"You were miles away then. Where were you?"

She blushed slightly, "I keep thinking about you getting involved with this memorial notice."

"I'll be fine, Sly."

They sat at the small round kitchen table with their coffee.

"I really wish that you would just forget all about it. But I know you; you won't consider my wishes and will just do your own thing."

He reached across and squeezed her hand.

"So what are you planning to do next?" She sighed.

"The first thing I have to do is discover who Ernie is."

"Why don't you ask Alice? She might have taken the order."

"Good thinking, Batman."

"What?"

"Never mind."

They finished their coffees in silence and Sylvia stood up from her chair.

"Well I'm off to work."

"Okay."

"See you later?" she said as a question rather than a goodbye.

"Yes I need to pop in at some time."

5

Alice Reeves had only been its Receptionist for seventeen months but knew the Newspaper as if she had worked there for years. Jack approached the Reception Desk and just as he was about to speak the telephone rang and a hand, palm facing him, stopped the conversation before he could start. Once the call was finished, Alice turned towards him.

"Good morning, Jack, can I help you?"

"I hope so, Alice. Tell me, do you take all the orders for advertisements, obituaries and the like?"

"If the customer comes in to us personally then, yes, otherwise orders by telephone or by post go straight to Derek's offices."

Jack took the crumpled piece of paper he still had in his pocket out and laid it on the desk.

"Do you know anything about this?"

Alice looked at it and then back to Jack. "Yes, the lady from Yorkshire."

"A lady, not the Ernie mentioned here?"

"No, but in a way yes."

Jack gave her an inquisitive look.

"Let me explain," she continued, "A lady said she was telephoning on behalf of Mr Mitchell."

"Mr Mitchell, not Mr Hall?"

"No, definitely not Hall but I remember this person because it was on the day that our telephone system went faulty and I couldn't transfer any of the calls. I had to deal with them in the best way that I could which was very difficult because the line was really bad. Not only that, Jack, but she had a very broad Yorkshire accent and to be honest, I found it rather difficult to fully understand everything she said. Anyway, she was telephoning on behalf of Mr Mitchell, I'm sure she said Mitchell, who wanted to place his usual memoriam notice in the Obituaries as he had done previously. This was a few weeks before the notice appeared because he wanted to settle his invoice in time for it to be entered. I explained the problem we had with our system then took a few details and told her someone would telephone back as soon as possible. I passed her details through to the office."

"Do you remember any of the details?"

"Not really but Derek sorts out invoices and accounts, I'm sure he'll be able to confirm the name and tell you anything else you want to know."

Shit chance, Jack thought to his self, *I won't get any help there.* Derek Mills did not like Jack Duggan one little bit.

"So, if you're right, I guess Ernie could well be Ernest, Ernest Mitchell then. Was there an address for him?"

"Actually I do remember the name of the place but I don't know if I am allowed to say. You know, confidentiality and all that"

"I work for the paper, Alice."

"Yes but," she looked round as if someone might be listening over her shoulder, and then continued. "The only thing I know is that the lady said she was phoning from The Watermill Rest Home."

"And The Watermill Rest Home is in Yorkshire?"

"Well, she didn't say Yorkshire but if her accent was a local one then, yes it could well be Yorkshire. But, as I said, Derek will be able to tell you more because he will have all the relevant details."

"What about a telephone number?"

"Derek will have that as well."

"Thank you Alice." He pointed towards the office door situated behind the Reception Desk. "I'm just popping through to see Sylvia."

"Hope I've been able to help."

Jack smiled at her and gave a nod as he went through the doorway.

In her office Sylvia had to refuse Jack's unethical request.

"Not a chance, Jack. Derek keeps his side of the business locked up tight; no one can access his department." Sylvia said abruptly.

"Typical of that…"

"Jack, don't be rude. Derek's a lovely man."

"He's a tosser." Jack muttered to himself.

"What is it you particularly want?"

"I've just spoken to Alice and it seems likely that Ernie could well be Ernest Mitchell and he probably lives in a residential home called The Watermill Rest Home in Yorkshire."

"Where in Yorkshire is it?"

"She didn't know."

"Bring over one of those chairs," she said, gesturing across the office. "I'll try Directory Enquiries."

Jack sat beside her as she dialled 192.

"Hello, the best I can do is Yorkshire, I'm afraid." And Sylvia asked for The Watermill Rest Home. Then, after a moment… "The Watermill Rest Home, Addlesdale, Yorkshire," and a telephone number followed. Sylvia jotted down the information as Jack looked at the note pad.

"That's it Sly, that's the one. Well done you."

"Don't get too excited Jack, there might be others that are not listed."

"I doubt places like that would be ex-directory. No, it's the one. Can I have that, Sly?"

He gave her a hug as she passed him the sheet from the pad.

"I don't know what I'd do without you."

"I hate to think, Jack Duggan, I really do hate to think."

6

The Watermill Rest Home, Addlesdale, Yorkshire was indeed the one, and by coincidence the lady who answered the telephone to him was the same person who had requested the invoice. Jack could also see what Alice Reeves meant by a 'broad Yorkshire accent'. She was reluctant to give any information unless he was a relative so Jack reeled off the story he had invented.

"Well I may be a relative but I don't know for sure. You see, the Charles Hall in that Memoriam was my Grandfather and I believe Billy Hall, the person who originally placed the Memorium, may have been my father. I say believe because my mother was divorced and would never talk about him. We lived on our own, never having any contact with other family. Indeed, I don't know whether there are any other family. Since she died I have started to search for him and I also want to be re-united with any family that there may be. When I saw the Memoriam Notice I wanted to get in touch with Mr Hall, hoping that he might indeed be my father but unfortunately he has passed away. Because Ernest Mitchell now places the Notice I am really hoping that he is a relation or at the very least can tell me something. I am really desperate to find out anything I can."

If she had just taken time to think about what Jack had told her she would have realised that names, dates and ages didn't add up at all. But as it was, she seemed to be taken in.

"Well, I'm not sure what his connection is to the person in the Memoriam and don't really know if he will be able to help you. For a start, I think you have the wrong person because our Ernest's name is not Mitchell its Whittall, Ernest William Whittall."

There was a moment's silence. Ernest William Whittall, E W Whittall; surely it couldn't be.

"Mr Duggan, are you still there?"

"Sorry, yes I was just checking my file as you were speaking. It's all beginning to make a lot more sense because I have a Whittall family noted here," he lied, "Look, I'm coming up to Yorkshire on business. Could I possibly come in and see him?"

"I'm afraid Ernest is very ill. He doesn't see anybody these days."

"If I call anyway, perhaps he might."

"I…"

"As I said I'm really desperate and this might be my last ever chance."

"If you ring back later, Mr Duggan, I'll see what I can do for you."

But Jack wasn't going to wait to see what she could do. He would be on the first train to Yorkshire early the next morning.

Her badge read 'Mrs Armstrong, Matron' but her looks were not the comforting image of a Matron; the stern voice certainly was not.

"I am not at all happy about this, Mr Duggan. You have disregarded any respect for this establishment, its guests and its rules. Quite frankly, no matter how far you've come, I should demand that you leave immediately. But I have been told of your desperation to find family and I know that our Mr Whittall wonders what happened to his family after the war. So for that reason and that reason alone I will allow you a few minutes with him."

She led Jack along a short corridor and stopped outside a closed door.

"Mr Whittall is very ill. He sleeps most of the time, so you may not get any information at all. In fact, he might not even know you're here. I'll call back in a short while and if I think he is at all stressed you will leave immediately. Is that understood Mr Duggan?"

"Yes Matron and thank you very much for this opportunity."

She opened the door and Jack followed her into the room eager to catch his first glimpse of Ernest William Whittall.

In a large comfortable bed lay a frail, white haired man. Clean crisp covers were pulled up to his neck and his eyes were closed. He was, as the Matron said he would be, fast asleep.

"Ernie, dear, there's a Mr Duggan here to see you. He's come a long way to ask you about family," she gestured Jack towards a chair. "As I told you, Mr Duggan, he's asleep. I'll be back in a little while."

"Thank you again for this chance, Matron."

After she had left and closed the door Jack pulled the chair up closer to the bed. Ernest Whittall's eyes remained closed and there was no sign at all of any realisation that there was someone in the room. Jack sat down, then leaned gently across and spoke quietly to the old man.

"Hello Mr Whittall, my name is Jack Duggan and I'm afraid I've told a few untruths because I'm not here to talk about family." Still there was no change in the old man's expression. "I've come here from the Isle of Sheppey in Kent to ask you about the memoriam notice for Charles Hall and why you placed it each year after Billy Hall died. I am also a great fan of your books, The Island Gang, and want to ask you about them." Jack took a little gamble. "I just wondered if there might be a connection between the two." And he sat back in his chair.

Slowly a smile spread across the frail old face and his eyes opened. The old man struggled to pull himself up in the bed and to turn towards Jack.

"Mr Duggan, I have waited a very long time for you to come."

A look of total surprise crossed Jack's face.

"I'm sorry, Mr Whittall, but how could you possibly know that I would be coming?"

"Because, I invited you; many years ago."

Jack stiffened in his seat, stunned by what he had heard. Following the silence of confusion Jack's voice raised an octave or two as he asked. "You invited me?"

The old man looked at the puzzled expression on Jack's face and smiled. "Well, Mr Duggan, Jack, may I call you Jack?"

"If I can call you Ernest"

"Ernie, please."

"OK, Ernie it is. But what do you mean 'you invited me, many years ago'?"

Ernie Whittall side stepped the question. "Tell me Jack, how is The Isle of Sheppey these days?"

"It's all right, but you still haven't answered my question."

"I will in good time, trust me. But for now, you have not properly answered my question."

"The Island is fine although some places are no longer what they were in their heyday."

"But, still a lovely place and still very interesting?"

"Yes, it will always be interesting."

"I'm glad to hear it"

"How long did you live there, Ernie?"

"Actually, I was only there for a very short time."

"But, by your stories, you gave the impression that you knew the Island very well."

"Oh indeed I did, Jack. In the very short time I was there I learnt much about the Island and its history." He looked Jack up and down. "So, I would guess you are a reporter."

"Yes, I'm afraid so."

"But not a national newspaper though?"

"No."

Still looking him up and down, "You work for Sheppey's local paper?"

Jack momentarily felt uncomfortable.

"Well, you must be devilishly good."

Jack shrugged his shoulders.

"You got past the armed guard." And Ernie nodded towards the door. He kept staring at Jack. "But are you good enough to hear and believe what I have to tell you? And are you good enough to use it wisely?"

Jack leaned back in the chair. "I don't know, Ernie, what is it that you have to tell me?"

"Something that is totally unbelievable."

"Unbelievable?"

"Yes, a story that could make your career Jack Duggan, just like Watergate did for Woodward and Bernstein," he said excitedly and then added. "If they ever let you tell it, that is."

"So this is about a scandal of some sort then." Jack suggested. "And who is it that won't let me tell the story, Ernie? You obviously don't mean Woodward and Bernstein, so who?"

Ernie ignored Jack's question and continued. "A story about people who are not who they say they are. About clues from the past telling of things in the future, or perhaps they were accurate predictions that have come true. Maybe they were lucky guesses…"

The door to the room opened and in walked the Matron. A look of surprise crossed her face as she saw Ernie sitting up in bed and chattering away.

"Well, Ernie, this is nice to see. Are you comfortable?" She fluffed up and adjusted pillows then tucked in bedding around him.

"I'm fine thank you Matron. Mr Duggan and I are having a wonderful discussion about families."

"As long as you don't get too tired I'll leave the both of you in peace." She looked at Jack with a face that seemed to be not quite so stern. "Mr Duggan, please be aware that Mr Whittall has been unwell. I will trust you not to stay too long, you can come back and see him again tomorrow."

"You can rely on me Matron and thank you."

Once she had left the room, Ernie was the first to speak.

"Talk to me about my books."

"What happened to the so called unbelievable story?"

"Talk to me about my books." He repeated.

"Ok, if that's what you want." Jack sat thinking for a while. "Where do you want me to start?" again he paused and when Ernie Whittall remained silent Jack continued. "When I was a child I loved books, I loved being dragged into their worlds. My favourites were what they called at that time 'Boys Own' type stories 'William and the Outlaws', 'Jennings and Darbishire' and of course the daredevil pilot 'Biggles'. I read a lot of the classic children's books, 'Treasure Island' and the like, but the ones I could really connect with were your stories about 'The Island Gang'.

"Children's books in those days were rather…How can I say? Rather 'jolly hockey sticks' and 'nice', if you know what I mean. Even though he was very mischievous and roguish like we were as kids, the parents of William Brown seemed very middle class as opposed to working class like my parents. Don't get me wrong, Ernie, they are all wonderful books and I love them as much now as I did then. But your books somehow portrayed the characters and events in a…I don't know, I suppose I'm trying to say 'in a more working class way'. And of course, living on Sheppey, I was there. It was all happening around me."

"Yes, I know exactly what you mean. And yes you're right, I did try to make them exactly what they were, working class Londoners, and keep the stories in that context. But you also have to remember that in those times there were certain expectations in literature so I had to pitch the stories at an acceptable standard for publication" He paused momentarily. "So tell me Jack, did you read all of my stories?"

"Yes, all six."

"When did you last read them?"

"The last time was many years ago, as a child."

"Have you still got the books?"

"Well, to be honest, I threw all my books out as I grew older. But over the last few years I came to realise how stupid that was, so have gradually been hunting down copies of all my favourite books through old book shops and antique shops. I've managed to collect many of them now and just recently discovered a set of all six Island Gang books. I haven't had chance to re-read them yet but I've brought them with me and would love it if you would sign them for me."

"It will be pleasure, Jack, where are they?"

Jack took the books from his case and passed them over. He also handed him a pen and with a very shaky hand Ernie signed all six.

"Apart from the Publishers first edition copies which I still have somewhere, these are the only copies I have seen for a very long time," he continued to look at the books. "So you haven't read these stories since your childhood?"

"No, like I said, I haven't had a chance since I found them."

"As I told you, Jack, the story I have to tell is totally unbelievable and I swear, on anything that you want me to swear on, it is the absolute truth. But I know that if I were to tell it now you would think I was an insane old man who had lost his marbles. Well I can assure you that my marble tin is full to overflowing, Jack, so to help you believe I need you to do something for me."

Jack exhaled sharply. "What?"

"Mr Duggan this is extremely serious. If you are not up to the task you might just as well leave now" Ernie Whittall said in an abrupt voice and then added in a more gentle tone. "Trust me please, Jack. I need you to believe."

"Ok, what do you want me to do?"

"Settle yourself into somewhere comfortable and then have a relaxing evening reading my books," he stared hard at Jack. "But do not read them 'as a child'. You must read them 'as an adult'."

"How do I read them as an adult?"

"Do not read the story. Read the words."

The two men looked into each other's eyes, Jack to see if the old man was just plain crazy. Ernie wanted to see whether Jack Duggan was starting to believe enough to go and study the books or whether he would simply leave the room and never come back.

Neither was sure about the other.

"I'm feeling tired now, Jack. Come back tomorrow and we can continue our conversation."

Ernie Whittall slid down into his bed clothes and closed his eyes. Jack moved the chair back to the other side of the room. He quietly opened the door and left. As he was closing the door, a tired voice came from within the room.

"How is the gorgeous Sylvia Stevens these days?"

He was just about to charge back into the room when another voice, this time from the hallway, stopped him.

"Thank you for not staying too late, Mr Duggan. Is Mr Whittall alright?"

"Yes, he is sleeping again."

"It was lovely to see him bright and alert; you're obviously the tonic he needs. I'll just pop in to see if he is comfortable. Will we see you again tomorrow?"

"Oh yes, Matron, you definitely will."

7

Sylvia had waited all day to hear from him. When the call finally came a very tentative voice said: "Hello Sly"

"Jack, where the hell are you?"

"I've just booked into a small pub for a couple of nights."

"Where?"

"The Red Lion."

"Very funny, Jack. You know what I mean. Whereabouts are you?"

"Well actually I'm in Yorkshire, Addlesdale to be exact."

"You could have told me you were going."

"Sorry Sly, I just did it on impulse."

"So I take it that you went looking for Mr Mitchell."

"Yes."

"Did you find him?"

"Well yes, but actually his name is not Mitchell, its Whittall. Ernest William Whittall." He paused to see if Sylvia responded to the name. When she didn't Jack continued. "He wrote books under the name of E W Whittall." Again he stopped.

"What sort of books?"

"Stories for children, which were all based on Sheppey."

Still Sylvia gave no hint of recognition.

"Not stories that I've read, Jack. I can't say I've ever heard of him or his books."

"That's funny, Sly, because he knows you."

"What do you mean?" she asked and sounded genuinely shocked.

"He knows you." Jack repeated.

"How does he know me?"

"I don't know, Sly." Jack replied and gave her a brief account of his meeting with Ernie Whittall, ending with him asking about her.

"Honestly, Jack, I don't recall the name or the person."

"Well, he certainly must have seen you because he knows you are gorgeous."

"Smoothy."

They carried on talking for a while and eventually Jack said he

31

had to go.

"I've got some books to read."

"Just be careful what you get up to, Jack, if not for your sake at least for mine."

"Bye Sly."

As she put down the telephone receiver Sylvia Stevens hoped that the 'bye' was not permanent.

After speaking to Sylvia, Jack had a shower and then settled himself down with the six books that each now contained the autograph of E W Whittall.

By the time he had reached halfway through 'Book One - The Island Gang' - Jack had been drawn, well and truly, back to his childhood. He was there with Maurice, Michael, James, Penny and June. Memories of the stories came flooding back.

'But do not read them as a child. You must read them as an adult. Do not read the story. Read the words'. Jack closed the book.

"Read the words, is what he said so let's give it a try." He mumbled to himself as he reopened Book One at the beginning.

Jack found that it wasn't at all simple to just look at the words without slipping into the stories, but then he noticed something that couldn't be right and it suddenly became a lot easier.

The Island Gang – Book One: The Island Gang. (1947)

Jack went through the first story but nothing unusual jumped out at him although he did make a mental note of something that he had never really thought about before but now it did seem rather a coincidence.

The Island Gang – Book Two: Smugglers Abound. (1948)

Chapter One.

Maurice Stevens pulled down the window of the carriage door. The smell of smoke from the steam train filled his nostrils as he leant out of the window.

"Maurice, don't lean out of the window, you'll get your head knocked off." A concerned Mrs Stevens called to him.

Maurice moved back a little way but continued to stretch out so that he could see the track ahead starting its gentle curve, a curve which would bring the black, smoking locomotive into view. He also knew that this curve meant the train would soon be approaching the four large concrete pillars of the bridge that would take them onto the Isle of Sheppey and he could already see them in the distance.

It wouldn't be long now before he met up again with Michael, James, Penny and June, The Island Gang. Hopefully there would be another great adventure, just like the one they had last year.

Jack picked up his notebook and a pen, then returning to Book One again he re-read the opening chapter.

Chapter One.

Maurice Stevens pulled down the window of the carriage door. The smell of smoke from the steam train filled his nostrils as he leant out of the window.

"Maurice, don't lean out of the window, you'll get your head knocked off." A concerned Mrs Stevens called to him.

Maurice moved back a little way but continued to stretch out so that he could see the track ahead starting its gentle curve, a curve which would bring the black, smoking locomotive into view. He also knew that this curve meant the train would soon be approaching the four large concrete pillars of the bridge that would take them onto the Isle of Sheppey and he could already see them in the distance.

Maurice didn't feel the usual excitement about the holiday this year, because at the age of ten he felt that now he was too old for sand castles, paddling pools and the Children's Club. Well, he was due to start Secondary School after the school holidays, he was grown up now. His mum and dad didn't seem to understand and had told him not to be so daft; there would be lots of things to do. He hoped so or it was going to be a very boring week. Maurice Stevens had no idea what this week had in store for him.

Jack started to make notes. He returned to Book Two and moved further into the story.

James saw the girls coming through the gardens.

"They're back." He shouted to Maurice and Michael. "Come on." and the boys ran over to greet them.

"Did you see him?" Michael asked.

"We couldn't see Sam Dixon at first but we saw his little boat, the 'Ferrio Lau'." June said excitedly.

"In the same place we saw it yesterday?" Maurice asked.

"Yes." Penny continued the report. "The tide is out so we walked out on the sand bank with a lot of other people to disguise ourselves."

"Well done, that was clever thinking" said Maurice. "What did you see?"

"Being out there we could see further along the coastline. The boat is parked..."

"Moored," Michael butted in.

"What?"

"Cars and lorries and buses are parked. Boats are moored." Michael corrected her.

"Alright smarty pants. Sam Dixon's boat is moored in a tiny gap just past where the old war boom goes out into the sea."

"What's a war boom?" James enquired with a puzzled look on his face.

"It's that row of old wrecked barges and posts that goes out into the sea." Maurice answered the question.

"What's it for?" James continued his enquiry.

"During the war a row of old barges and wooden posts were sunk into the mud as a trap for any submarines that might try to sneak along the coast."

"Are there any submarines stuck in it now?"

"No, of course there aren't."

"Oh." James sounded disappointed.

"Can we get round there?" Michael changed the subject.

"Probably but we would have to be careful. The mud can be dangerous especially when the tide comes in." June advised.

"Yes, but those two men got round there." Penny quickly pointed out.

"What two men?" Maurice, Michael and James asked, almost in one voice.

"Well, you didn't give me chance to finish." Penny said sulkily.

"We are all very sorry, Penny." The boys all said together. "Carry on please."

"We noticed two men, who seemed to be in a hurry, go along the bottom of the cliffs, across the mud. When they reached the boat, we could see Mr Dixon come out from the cabin. Although it was *quite a way away from us we think he gave each of the men a package because they were carrying something as they worked their way back across the mud then both men went up the cliffs."*

"Is the boat still there?" asked Maurice.

"Yes because it can't go anywhere until the tide comes in." Penny added smugly.

"Cool." Maurice smiled. "We better not go over the mud so let's walk along the cliffs and investigate."

Book Three started in the same way as Book Two with Maurice Stevens approaching the bridge.

The Island Gang – Book Three: A Spy in The Camp. (1949)

They had been watching the mysterious man for two days now.

"Warners will never believe that they have a spy hiding in one of their chalets." The Island Gang said amongst themselves.

"I'm going to listen at his window. I might hear something valuable." Michael said.

"Take Penny with you. If anyone asks what you are doing just say that you are playing hide and seek." Maurice advised.

"OK." And they both left.

The others followed at a safe distance.

Being in the farthest corner of the third row behind the paddling pool his chalet was far enough away from the grassed area to be reasonably quiet. Usually it was only the holidaymakers staying in that last chalet who were found along there.

The door of the chalet flew open.

"What do you two think you are doing?"

"We're playing hide and seek." Michael and Penny gave their prepared excuse.

"No you're not. You were listening at my window." The man looked quickly about then grabbed them both roughly and dragged them into the chalet.

The rest of the gang looked on with alarm from the end of the row.

"What do we do now?" June wanted to know.

"I don't know." Maurice said. "Let me think."

The same Chapter as the previous books opened Book Four.

The Island Gang – Book Four: A Ghost on the Track. (1950)

"It's gone." James shouted excitedly as he entered the gangs meeting place. "The train has gone."

Gradually, during the afternoon Maurice, Michael, Penny and June had gathered, as they had done each year for the last three years, in their secret meeting place and now the arrival of James completed the members of the Island Gang. James gabbled on without taking a breath.

"It blew up with a big explosion on Christmas Day and there were hundreds killed and now there's a ghost."

Maurice, being the eldest and most sensible of the five, put him right.

"It did not blow up, James. The light railway has simply been closed down; it was during December but not on Christmas Day. There was no big explosion and no-one has been killed.

"But there is a ghost." James argued, trying hard to save a bit of his exaggerated story.

"There's no such thing as ghosts." Penny said, shuddering.

"Yes there is," James insisted. "A man told my dad that strange things have been happening and awful noises heard along the track. Some people have seen a dark, shadowy figure floating along the line."

"Where was that?" asked Michael.

"Don't tell me you believe all that rubbish, Michael?" June laughed.

"No, I don't believe in ghosts, but perhaps something mysterious is happening. We should investigate."

Book five also began with that same opening chapter.

The Island Gang – Book Five: Treasure in the Grounds. (1951)

Written on the old torn piece of paper was a clue.

"What is it a clue to?" asked Maurice

"Treasure." James shouted

"It doesn't say treasure." Penny said, sarcastically.

"Clues always lead to treasure." James argued back.

"No they don't...

"Let's try to find the next clue and see what it says." Maurice

suggested. "What does the clue say, James?"

As the book continued The Island Gang gradually found and solved further clues which eventually lead them on a trail along Minster cliffs and through Minster Village. After crossing the cliffs again, towards Warden the gang ended up at a large house in private grounds.

A big sign on the gate read PRIVATE KEEP OUT. Maurice, Michael, James, Penny and June pushed their noses to the railings of the gates, trying to see in as far as possible.
"We need to get in," said James "Cos that's where the treasure is."
"I keep telling you, there isn't any treasure." Penny once again informed him.
"If there isn't any treasure why would the clues bring us here?"
Before the argument could go any further a loud voice suddenly boomed out.
"Clear off you nosey kids. This is private property."
The gang stepped back from the gate.
"Go on, clear off, NOW." The old man, approaching the gate, screamed at them.
"Who was that?" Michael asked as they walked away.
"I don't know." Maurice answered.
"He must be a Lord or something, living in a big house like that." June suggested.
"More like a lunatic, shouting and screaming about at everyone." Penny added.
James put forward the final conclusion "A screaming Lord who is such a loony." And they all laughed in agreement.
They decided that they would come back later and try to get into the grounds of the big house. Then they would search to see what mysteries the clues would reveal.

Like the previous stories Book Six also began with Maurice Stevens looking out of the train window as it approached the Island.

The Island Gang - Book Six: The Final Chase. (1952)

With three prisons on the Island there had to be an escape at some time. Plans were put into operation and the bridge had been raised to stop anyone getting off the Island, but equally it also stopped anyone getting on. The search process was set in place.

"You mean we won't be able to go home, ever." A worried June asked.

"Yes," James said excitedly. "We will have to stay here for the rest of our lives, having adventures and solving mysteries."

June started to look worried.

"Don't worry, June," Maurice smiled. "The bridge will only be up for a while. Just until the escaped prisoner is found or until the road, going off the Island, can be guarded properly."

"Let's go and tell the Police that we want to help." Michael said.

"No, they will only tell us to keep away. So I think we will have to do our own searching." Suggested Maurice and everyone agreed.

Finally Jack reached what was not only the end of the story but also the end of The Island Gang.

As the train took the Stevens family off the Island at the end of yet another holiday Maurice looked out over the Swale. The sadness he felt was not only for the end of another adventurous holiday but for the fact that it was also the end of The Island Gang. He had left school at the start of the summer holiday and would now, at the age of fifteen, be going to work at the Factory with his dad. Also, his parents had been talking about going somewhere different for a holiday next year. Perhaps they might try the new Butlins camp down on the south coast.

The gang had decided that like the Three Musketeers they were 'All for one and one for all' so unless they were five the Island Gang would be no more. He hoped that one day he would meet up again with Michael, James, Penny and June. Perhaps, then they could investigate things again just like the American Private Eyes he had seen in films.

"We will have to wait and see." He said aloud.

"What, love?"

"Nothing, Mum."

Eventually Jack put down the books and dropped into a deep sleep for the rest of what was now a very short night.

The ringing of the bedside telephone woke him, he quickly looked at his watch then picked up the receiver; he knew who it would be.

"Good morning Sly."

"Jack, are you alright"

"I'm fine, just a bit tired."

"Oh yes, and what have you been up to Mr Jack Duggan?"

"Other than spending the whole night with a set of books I have nothing exciting to report Ma'am."

"Oh yes, I remember you saying. Children's stories weren't they?"

"Yes."

"So was there anything of interest in them?"

"I think there might well be. I need you to find out some things for me urgently, Sly. Can you get back to me as soon as possible this morning before I go to see Ernie Whittall? You can fax it all to me here at The Red Lion; they will let me know when it arrives." And Jack gave her the fax number.

"Never mind all the work that I'm paid to do, I'll just push everything aside for you Jack Duggan." She said reminding him that she was actually at work.

"Thank you, Miss Stevens. Honestly though, it is important Sly, there are definitely things that don't add up here and I hope your answers to my questions will give me the ammunition to tackle Mr Whittall."

"So what do you want to know?"

"First, get hold of two pictures for me. I need a picture of the Kingsferry lifting Bridge that we have now, also a picture of the previous bridge. It must be the bridge that would have been in use during the 1940s, especially 1947. Then can you find out the following information for me."

Jack went over the things that had caught his attention in the books and then repeated the fax number in case Sylvia had missed it the first time.

"As quick as you can, Sly."

"Yes Sir."

"Please."

"OK, I'm on it."

"Thanks Sly."

Jack enjoyed a hearty breakfast and then carried a large cup of coffee through to the Bar. He made himself comfortable at a table in the far corner of the room and set about sorting through his notes from the previous night and making more notes, ready for his meeting with Mr E W Whittall.

At twenty past ten, several pages arrived in the office of The Red Lion Public House via their fax machine.

8

The Matron who met Jack when he entered the Waterside Rest Home this time was completely different from the Matron who was so sharp and stern with him yesterday. Although the same person, today her face had a soft glow.

"Good morning Jack," she greeted him with a gentle, warm voice and a welcoming smile. "You certainly had an impact on our Ernest. He has been up and eagerly awaiting your visit. You better go on through."

"Good morning Matron, thank you."

Jack walked along the hallway and when he reached the door to Ernie Whittall's room he knocked gently.

"Come in." A voice from inside summoned.

Jack opened the door and peered round it to find, not a frail old man lying in his bed but a washed, shaved and sharply dressed man looking fresh and alert sitting in a large comfortable chair. Beside the chair stood a small table with a cup of tea upon it and another chair similar to the one in which Ernie Whittall now sat.

"Come on in, Jack, it's good to see you again." He slowly stood and offered his hand, which Jack shook. "Would you like a cup of tea or coffee?"

"Hello Ernie. No thank you very much, but you carry on with yours." He released Ernie's hand and Ernie sat back down. "This is a bit of a change from yesterday. You look extremely well."

"I feel very good thank you and I've been waiting for you to come back, although I wasn't sure if you would."

"Oh, why was that?"

"I wondered whether, after our meeting yesterday you might just have thought I was a mad old man and boarded the first train back down south."

"To tell you the truth, Ernie, that is exactly what I intended to do until you called out to me just as I left your room."

Ernie's face broke into an almost triumphant smile.

"Anyway, come on, sit down." He gestured towards the empty chair. Jack laid the envelope he was carrying, along with his note book, pen and pocket tape recorder on the table and sat down.

41

"Hello, what's all this?"

"Some questions."

"Interesting."

Jack settled back in the empty chair and then looking across at the old man sitting in the other chair. "So tell me Ernie, are you some sort of modern day soothsayer character with your prophecies for the future hidden in stories?"

Ernie Whittall laughed out loud. "I wish I was, Jack, but no, I cannot predict what the future has in store for us all."

"But you do seem to have had the ability to write certain things into your stories which you could not possibly have known about at the time."

"Have I? And what things would they be?"

Jack leaned forward and picked up the envelope that he had laid on the table when he first sat down. Opening it he took out the contents and laid them beside himself, except for one picture which he put on the table in front of Ernie. Then he opened his note book.

"Last night I did as you said. I booked myself into a local establishment."

"The Red Lion?"

"Yes, as it happens, it was the Red Lion."

"Lovely place, I used to visit their bar regularly when I was more able. How's the barman, Tom I think it was. How is he these days?"

"I don't know, I didn't see a barman. There was a young lady serving behind the bar last night."

"Oh."

"Anyway, as I was saying, I settled into The Red Lion and then had an evening with your books."

"And?"

"By half way through Book One I was back into my childhood…"

"Oh dear."

"By half way through Book One I was back into my childhood," Jack repeated and then continued. "But then I remembered what you had said. So I started again, trying to see the words rather than the story and I began to notice things.

"I suppose at first I hadn't quite got the hang of looking at the words and disassociating them from the others around them so by the end of Book One I had seen nothing that made me look twice. There was one thing that struck me as rather a coincidence though. But I'll come back to that later."

Jack reached across to pick up the photograph that he had laid on the table and passed it to Ernie

"That is the only way onto the Isle of Sheppey by road or rail at the time of you writing your books."

"Yes, that's right." Ernie agreed.

"At the start of Book Two, which was written in 1948, something did make me look twice." Jack picked up his notes. "In the opening chapter you wrote about Maurice approaching the Island. You said ' He also knew that this curve meant the train would soon be approaching the four large concrete pillars of the bridge that would take them onto the Isle of Sheppey and he could already see them in the distance'. I re-checked Book One, written in 1947, because it struck me that the beginning was the same. Well, it was similar but not quite the same because obviously Maurice had not yet met The Island Gang. But Book Three from 1949, Four from 1950, Five 1951 and Six 1952 did all have that same opening chapter." Jack pointed to the photograph Ernie was still holding. "I cannot see any large concrete pillars on that bridge, can you?" When there was no reply from Ernie, he passed a second photograph over the table. "But there is no doubt about the four large concrete pillars to the structure of this bridge."

Ernie Whittall looked briefly at the photograph and smiled.

"And those are the pillars in my stories."

"But how can they be when that picture you are looking at is of the present Kingsferry Bridge which did not come into use until 1960."

"Opened on 20th April 1960 by the Duchess of Kent; if I remember rightly." Ernie added.

"So how could you write about it in 1947?"

Ernie leaned back in his chair.

"Come on, Ernie, when are going to start telling me something?"

"When you are ready, Jack, I promise."

Jack shook his head and picked up his notes.

"One thing that I nearly missed in Book Two was Sam Dixons boat the Ferio Lau. Was that the Ferry Olau, a play on the Olau ferry?"

"Well spotted, Jack, I'm impressed."

"The Olau ferry operated between Sheerness and Vlissingen, in Holland, during the 1970s, 1980s and 1990s. That is why I talk about seeing into the future because how else could you have known about it?"

"As I said before, I do not have the ability to tell you what the future has in store."

"But you have to admit that there are things in your stories that must seriously make me think otherwise."

"Perhaps you are right, so tell me more about those things then, Jack."

"I feel like I'm banging my head against a brick wall here." Jack muttered as he referred to his notes again. "Also in Book Two, and I noticed it dotted around in most books, was Maurice's use of the word 'cool' which I didn't think was an expression of those times. More 1960s and 70s I would have thought?"

A raise and lower of his eyebrows were Ernie's only confirmation.

"In 1949, Book Three was called 'A Spy in The Camp' in which you wrote "Warners will never believe that they have a spy hiding in one of their chalets." The Island Gang said amongst themselves'."

"Yes" was all that Ernie offered.

"But Warners didn't open a Holiday Camp on the Island until sometime during the 1950s."

"In Minster-on-Sea, about 1954 I think." Ernie added.

"Of course we know that now but how on earth did you know there would be a Warners Holiday Camp five years before it existed?" Jack could feel the frustration starting to build when once again no explanation was offered by Ernie. He took a moment to calm himself down and then continued. "Book Four, A Ghost on the Track. I wasn't sure about that one because I didn't know the history of Sheppey's Light Railway. I needed a bit more information before I could tell whether there were things I needed to note," he paused momentarily. "I found out that the railway did actually close in December 1950 so at first I didn't think there was anything out of the ordinary. I pondered the point for a while because there had to be something, didn't there? Then I realised that the book was published during 1950 which means you wrote the story possibly late 1949 or early 1950. It turns out, once again, something happened that you could not have known about at the time of writing the story."

"Yes, I did leave that a bit tight but it was purely the fact that I couldn't remember exactly when during the 50s the railway actually closed."

"Couldn't remember?"

"That's right." was Ernie's only comment, and once more he leaned back into his chair and closed his eyes as he listened.

Again Jack shook his head. "In Book Five, Treasure in the Grounds, another subtle prediction…"

"Not prediction, Jack. There are no predictions."

"You keep saying that, but I certainly cannot see how they can be things you remembered. So until you tell me different, predictions they are."

"Suit yourself, Jack."

"As I was saying," He paused a moment. "In Book Five, Treasure in the Grounds, another subtle prediction jumped out at me. Actually no, you are right it was not a prediction. In this instance it was more like a very subtle reference to something, or rather someone. After The Gang had an encounter with a particularly grumpy house owner the story says that 'James put forward the final conclusion "A screaming Lord who is such a loony." And they all laughed in agreement', which struck me as a reference to Screaming Lord Sutch and The Raving Loony Party or Monster Raving Looney Party to give its full name."

"Once again, well spotted, and yes you are right, it was."

"Screaming Lord Sutch was a pop star in the 1960s, although his music was pretty weird. Then in 1964 he started the pirate radio station Radio Sutch which broadcast from the old abandon Shimmering Sands army fort, off the Essex coast. He is probably better known for founding The Monster Raving Loony political party in 1983, but of course you already seem to have known all about that back in 1951?"

"Well I couldn't have written anything about a loony these days, could I? Not 'Politically Correct' you know."

"But that's not an explanation."

"No, you're probably right."

Jack waited but again Ernie added nothing. Although Mr

Ernest William Whittall seemed to accept all the issues Jack pointed out, he hadn't actually given away anything that resembled an unbelievable story. Jack was now finding it more and more difficult to fight his irritation but once again managed to settle himself enough to carry on.

"In 1952 came Book Six, The Final Chase, in which you wrote 'With three prisons on the Island there had to be an escape at some time'. Of course, there are three prisons on the Isle of Sheppey now. But not in 1952 when there was only the one, Standford Hill. It was opened on the site of an old Royal Air force Station, just outside of Eastchurch, in 1950. Redevelopment of the site in the 1980s added Swaleside Prison and finally Elmley Prison in 1992." Ernie's eyes remained closed and Jack gave a large sigh before he continued. "Sadly Book Six brought stories about The Gang to a close but even in those dying moments you tucked in another little mystery. You wrote 'Also, his parents had been talking about going somewhere different for a holiday next year. Perhaps they might try the new Butlins camp down on the south coast'. If you were thinking about Butlins at Bognor Regis it would have been a bit difficult for them to go there the following year because that Butlins Camp didn't open until 1960." He placed his notes back on the little table. "So there you are Ernie, I've done my bit. Now how about you telling me what all this is about."

Ernie Whittall opened his eyes and looked across the table towards Jack, "You said in Book One there was something that struck you as rather a coincidence. What would that have been?"

"For God's sake, Ernie, this is starting to piss me off."

"Jack, please calm down."

I'll give him calm down if he says that again, Jack thought. "In Book One and of course in the others as well you gave Maurice's family the surname of Stevens."

"Yes."

"Yesterday, as I left your room, you called out to me 'How is the gorgeous Sylvia Stevens these days'..."

"You are going to ask me if giving them the surname of Stevens was a coincidence. Well it wasn't. I gave them that name as a reminder of Sylvia."

"A reminder of her in 1947?"

"Correct."

46

"In 1947 Sly, sorry Sylvia, would only have only been four years old so that can't be right either."

"But I didn't meet her in 1947; I met her many years later."

"What do you mean you met her many years later?" Jack almost shouted at Ernie. "None of this is making any sense at all." He leapt out of the chair and started picking up the photographs and notes. "You wrote stories that contained riddles…"

"Riddles, yes I like that." Ernie nodded his head.

"…riddles about things which did actually happen in the future, things that you could not possibly have known about at the time. I am trying to understand how you did that but you don't help me at all, you just keep stringing me along. You say that you have a story to tell but have told me absolutely nothing. You speak of knowing Sylvia Stevens back in the 1940s and then say you only met her many years later although she insists that she does not know you at all. I have no idea what's going on here but I can tell you that I'm fed up with all this bullshit, so I'm on the next train out of here. Goodbye Mr Whittall, meeting you has been…"

"Jack wait, listen a moment," Ernie shouted to him as he opened the door of the room. "Sylvia may think she does not know me but I can assure you that she does. Because, you see, Jack, she knows me as Phillip Easterbrook."

For the second time since he had met Ernie Whittall Jack was stunned. He stood halfway in and halfway out of the doorway.

"Phillip Easterbrook, you are Phillip Easterbrook?"

"Yes. Close the door, Jack, come back in and sit down."

Jack settled back down in the chair that he had leapt out of just a moment ago.

"Right, are you ready with your note book?"

"I have a recorder, Ernie. Do you mind if I use that?"

"No I don't mind at all."

Jack set up the recorder and stood it on the table beside Ernie. They did a quick introductory recording and after Jack checked that it had been successful he sat back in his chair. "So Ernie, you are telling me that you are not Ernest William Whittall but are actually Phillip Easterbrook?"

"No, I am telling you that I am both Ernest William Whittall and Phillip Easterbrook."

"What then," Jack thought for a moment. "Ernie Whittall

47

visits the Isle of Sheppey in the guise of Phillip Easterbrook, gets bored and disappears without a trace. No thought for the people left behind worrying and wondering about what happened to him."

"Well, no, it wasn't quite as simple or as blatant as that, Jack. You see, at that time I was Phillip Easterbrook. I didn't become Ernest William Whittall until later on."

"Don't you mean you became Phillip Easterbrook later on?"

"No, I mean exactly what I said."

"But that can't be right," Jack paused while he tried to work out what Ernie was saying. "You're talking in riddles again Ernie. So come on, tell me why things are not so simple."

Ernie rested back in his chair and Jack moved the recorder closer to the edge of the table.

"What I am about to tell you is going to sound utterly unbelievable and totally impossible. But once again I assure you that it is the absolute truth and I hope that what you've discovered and have just been talking to me about will start to make sense. More importantly I hope it will make you believe."

Ernie Whittall took a deep breath

"In the late 1960s I was involved in a terrible accident...

Part Two

The Second Beginning

9

In August of 1967 an explosion totally destroyed four houses in Bower Terrace and shattered windows in several streets around. Two adjacent houses that were damaged structurally eventually had to be demolished and the frontages of four houses on the opposite side of the street required substantial repair.

During the late 1960s The Gas Council began converting Britain, area by area, from coal gas to natural gas – initially known as North Sea gas - starting in and around Burton on Trent in Derbyshire. On the day of the changeover the process required every household in the chosen area to turn off all their gas appliances. Once this had been done the old coal gas was first removed from the system and then gas engineers went from house to house fitting the new parts required. When completed, natural gas was allowed to flow into the system.

The fact that natural gas has very different burning properties from coal gas meant many old appliances had to be converted or replaced for use with the new gas. It was thought that a misunderstanding of this situation by one elderly resident of Bower Terrace had caused a gas leak that resulted in the massive explosion. The Gas Council, and later British Gas, always refuted that theory because to them the explosion was far too big to be the result of a gas leak. Also, not only was there the 'explosion', but at the same time there also appeared to have been an 'implosion'. Their own theory was that the damage had been caused by an unexploded war time bomb or the houses had been struck by an object or objects unknown.

Number 37 had been dilapidated and empty for many years but seven people had lived in the other destroyed houses. Mr and Mrs Martin with Mrs Martin's elderly mother lived at number 31 while Mr and Mrs Easterbrook with their young son Phillip were at number 33 with Mrs Baker at number 35. Only two complete bodies were ever found. The first was Mrs Martin and she later died of extensive injuries. The second was a boy. Neighbours knew that the Easterbrook's had a son Phillip, so police were able to put a name to the person pulled from the wreckage. As he slowly regained consciousness it quickly became apparent that the serious head injuries sustained by this young man had wiped all memories of the explosion and his life prior to it.

Friends and neighbours would never see Phillip Easterbrook again. Cared for and brought up in several specialised homes, he recovered from the injuries but never regained any of his lost memory. As far as he was aware, his life started from the day he had been pulled from the wreckage of number 33 Bower Terrace.

10

For many decades, health problems relating to the brain were collectively grouped under the umbrella of 'Mental Health'.

The expression 'shell shock' was first coined during World War One when soldiers started to complain of dizziness, severe headaches, hypersensitivity to noise, tinnitus and, in some cases, amnesia. These conditions were indicative of exposure to explosions or head injuries caused by artillery shells. But the fact that complaints were also coming from soldiers who had not been injured or exposed to artillery explosions meant that physical damage could not be the sole cause. Doctors came to the view that perhaps shell shock was also the result of emotional injury.

Initially a hardened military refused to accept that 'emotional shell shock' existed and those men claiming so were branded as agitators and cowards. But by 1917 the British army's attitude had started to change and methods were introduced to reduce the symptoms that appeared to be caused emotionally. By late 1917 the number of men suffering from emotional shell shock had reduced dramatically. In some ways this had, unknowingly, been the forerunner of changes made to the way mental health would eventually be treated.

Over the decades mental health started to be dealt with differently. Health problems relating to the brain were gradually categorised with injury trauma being separated from emotional trauma. Rehabilitation began to be seen as the way forward.

During the 1960s and 1970s 'Case Management' was developed in the United States of America as a means of assessing the needs of mental health patients and their families. Dr Randolph Florrello had been involved with that scheme and in the late 1960s moved to Britain where he started to develop the system that would eventually be used here. While on a visit to The Derbyshire Royal Infirmary, he heard about a young boy who had been admitted to the Children's Hospital with severe head injuries sustained in an explosion. Treatment of those injuries had gone so much better than Doctors could ever expect but the boy's memory had been wiped clean. Dr Florrello immediately took to this young man and personally oversaw the rehabilitation of Phillip Easterbrook.

Those early days were very frightening for Phillip because he did not know who he was or where he was. Phillip Easterbrook had to re-learn everything from scratch, but eventually wounds healed and a damaged brain caught up with itself. Although he never did regain any memories of the accident or his life prior to it Phillip always felt that there was a connection to something, something he could not explain. If ever he spoke to anyone about it, he would liken the feeling to the expression 'something on the tip of your tongue'. It is frustratingly right there but just would not come out.

Now a brain previously wiped clean wanted to fill that space with information. Learning and education came easy to Phillip and he quickly surpassed those children who had started their schooling so many years earlier. Following a grammar school education the progression to University was just a formality.

Phillip studied journalism and following university he teamed up with Dr Florrello to publish papers and books on mental health including the work carried out in the U.S.A. and the early days of care by the NHS.

In 1986 Parkinson's disease which had been slowly creeping up on Randolph, gathered strength so he returned to America; accompanied by Phillip Easterbrook. The next two years revolved around 'A Different Type of Management', the autobiography of Dr Randolph Florrello.

Sadly, in 1989 Randolph Florrello passed away so Phillip returned to England where he decided to continue his career in writing. He found himself a quaint little house sited in a small hamlet on the Isle of Sheppey in Kent and settled down.

But now, without Randolph, Phillip found that he had lost the enthusiasm for medical subjects. He still wanted to write, so contacted the local newspaper and put forward the idea of writing short articles about the history of the island and people's memories of it. The young lady he spoke to thought the idea very interesting and suggested to her editor that they should give Phillip Easterbrook a trial. The editor agreed with Sylvia Stevens.

11

Jack Duggan leaned towards Ernie Whittall "So Sylvia first came to know you when you worked for our little outfit."

"Well, she was actually the one who suggested they employ me but yes, that was the start of my relationship with her."

"Relationship, how deep did this relationship go?"

"Mr Duggan, a gentleman never speaks of such things. However, as the word relationship seems to have hit a raw nerve with you I can safely say that Sylvia and I were just good friends and work colleagues."

"I didn't mean…"

"Please, Jack, just keep quiet and do not interrupt me again until I have completed my story," Ernie scolded him. "It is very complicated and I need to concentrate so that I remember everything. I want to relate every detail." Ernie wriggled in his chair to make himself comfortable again and closed his eyes. He remained silent for several minutes, to the point where Jack thought that perhaps Ernie had fallen asleep but after his telling off he did not dare try to find out. Eventually Ernie opened his eyes and continued.

"I really enjoyed those few years working for that newspaper. Jack, I'm glad we're agreed that the Isle of Sheppey is such an interesting place. It's full of wonderful history and wonderful people who, for the most part, have a story to tell and in that short time I met so many of them. I could talk forever about the place but I would be deviating from what I should be telling you."

He paused, deep in thought.

"During that time, I think in 1992, someone brought to my attention a Memoriam Notice for Charlie Hall which had been placed in the newspaper every year since the end of the war. I initially made a somewhat casual enquiry but no one seemed to know anything about it. Obviously there must have been other pressing things on my mind because I didn't proceed any further until I saw the same notice in the paper again the following year. I began to think there must be more to this and I started to sense an interesting story so decided I would like to interview Mr Hall. I finally called him in September 1993 and it went something like this:

'Hello, could I speak to Mr Billy Hall…'

'Charlie, oh my God, Charlie. Oh my God, I can't believe it after all these years. I just knew you weren't dead. Charlie it's me, Billy.'

'No Mr Hall my name is Phillip, Phillip Easterbrook.'

'Charlie, can't you feel us?'

"And I could feel something. It was like… like… it was as if… as if Billy Hall was reaching through the telephone and trying to pull me to him. And equally, it felt as if something in me was also reaching through to pull Billy Hall to me.

"A sharp pain shot through my head, my ears felt as if they would burst and a blinding light hurt my eyes, then darkness. The explosion, I could see and feel the explosion but more than that I could see beyond it. Darkness again and then through the darkness someone was calling: 'Charlie, what's happened? Where are you?'

"My head hurt and I could see the image of a young, scruffy boy dressed in a tatty shirt, grey short trousers and an old tank top type jumper. He had long socks that had dropped down around his ankles and he wore old boots. What was so strange about the image was that the scruffy boy was me, but it couldn't be me because I was looking at him. I couldn't work out what my head was doing. I think I stammered something about the need to see Billy urgently and I remember almost falling out of the door in my haste to go and see Billy Hall.

"I have to confess that I have no idea exactly how I managed to get there. My head had been taken over by images of a childhood unknown to me. There was I travelling from Sheerness in 1993 but all I could see were scenes of London and of war. Now I was on a train full of children, many of whom I knew, and next to me that same scruffy boy I had seen earlier. Suddenly it became clear; I must have been sitting on a train with my twin brother."

"Your twin brother," Although he had been told not to, Jack couldn't help the interruption.

Ernie glared at him and then continued.

"Finally the train stopped at a station and a few of us were told to get off. As we were led outside of the station there were no houses, in fact no buildings at all. Where was this place? Had the Germans got here first and blown everything up? I looked back and saw a sign which read WESTCOTT. What part of London was this?

"An old truck took us to a large wooden hut which had 'village hall' painted on the front. Here a rather stout man in a suit, who I thought looked like a school headmaster, boomed out 'Welcome to Westcott.' Where was this Westcott? What was this Westcott?

"Darkness again and then I realised I had managed to arrive safely at the house of Billy Hall. As I said before; how I managed it I do not know, I must have been driving in a trance.

"The door opened before I had chance to knock and stood there in the doorway was me, but an older me. There is no different way I can describe the person standing before me other than exactly that 'me, but an older me'. Apart from the obvious age difference our features were identical. Also, Jack, there was something else: that 'pull' again and now it had become incredibly strong.

Before I could speak Billy Hall stepped forward and grabbed me. Hugging me tight he was almost in tears.

'Charlie, oh my God Charlie it is you. I have waited so long for this moment. I knew they were wrong, I knew that you hadn't died.' And he hugged me again.

'Billy.' I gasped as his hug felt like he was trying to squeeze the breath out of me. He relaxed his hold and held me at arm's length.

'Let me have a look at you.' Billy eyed me up and down. 'Blimey, Charlie, you look so young.' Then pulling me close to him again he added. 'I just can't believe you've found me at last. Why did it take you so long? What happened and where have you been? Come on in and tell me all about it.'

I followed him into the house.

'Oh how I wish Mum was here to see this.' He paused a moment. 'Oh, I'm sorry Charlie; you probably don't know that Mum passed away.' And even though at this moment in time memories of my, of our, Mum were just a confused series of images flashing through my head a deep sadness welled up in my heart. 'No, I didn't.'

Billy broke the short period of silence.

'So come on Charlie sit down and tell me all about it.'

'Billy, I'm afraid I can't because I don't know. You see, up until the moment I spoke to you on the telephone I have been Phillip Easterbrook. My life and memories start from the day I survived a massive explosion…'

'I knew it. There was an explosion but they would never believe me.'

'Do you mean that you were there when the house exploded?'

'Not a house, Charlie. You disappeared when there was an explosion in an old hut that we got into.'

'No, I was found after an explosion in the house where I lived. It was 1967 and I was ten years old.'

'Yes, you were ten years old when you disappeared. But not in 1967, Charlie, you disappeared from that old hut in 1943.'

"My head was starting to hurt again. I needed to make sense of what Billy was telling me and what my head was now trying to tell me.

'Billy I think you should go ahead and tell me your side of the story and I'll try to make sense of all this.'

'A cup of tea first though.' Billy offered and he made towards the kitchen."

12

Billy and Charlie 1993.

Billy passed a mug to his guest then sat down in an armchair. Holding the mug with both hands he took a sip.

"You know, Charlie, life was rough in Bethnal Green but Mum and Dad brought us up right. Mum was tough as old boots but she was also loving and gentle. Dad worked in the docks, he was hard working and very strict; he kept us on the straight and narrow. Don't get me wrong, Dad never beat us or anything like that. He didn't have to; he just gave us that look, the look that let us know we would be in serious trouble if we disobeyed. Although, in saying that, we did get a couple of good hidings. Once when you nicked some sweets from old Davidson's shop and he couldn't tell which one of us took them so we both copped it. Another time was when we played truant from school, but I think we had learned our lesson and never dared to test him again.

"As twins, we may have been identical but our personalities were the exact opposites, like chalk and cheese. You were a rough and tumble type of kid, whereas I was always a bit soft and nervous."

"Scaredy Cat." The phrase suddenly came out.

"Yeh, so you remembered that then." Billy said, rather disappointedly.

"No. It just came to me then."

"Anyway, we were always there for each other. You looked after me and I might have been soft and nervous but if you were in trouble I was there beside you, against the biggest of them all. We got quite a reputation…oh nothing bad, it was just that kids knew we stood up for ourselves and they never gave us any bother.

"Then the war came and like loads of other kids we were evacuated. They sent us to a little place in Wiltshire."

"Westcott."

"Yes, that's right, Westcott. The train journey was awful, it took hours to get there which caused a lot of stress to us kids. And even then many of them still had to go a lot further before they arrived at where they were going.

"Everything was all a bit strange to us; we had never seen a place like it. The kids were all split up from each other and were sent off with different people. They told us that these were the people who we would be living with until it was safe to go home. I think some of the kids got real dodgy characters to stay with but we were all right. We would be staying with Mr and Mrs Philpott at their house on the edge of the village. The Philpotts were very kind but they had no idea how to sort kids out so we got away with murder, staying out late and getting up to all sorts of mischief. That was you again, Charlie. You always led me on."

"Me?"

"Yeh you. Anyway, the Philpotts never moaned at us, I think they sort of knew we wouldn't bring them any serious trouble and we quickly got used to our new surroundings. It was all very strange at first but eventually it was like a great adventure. The only downside was that we had to go to school but it still left plenty of time to have fun.

"We used to go up the Heath and into the woods…"

"Darkling Woods."

"Blimey, Charlie, I've been trying to remember the name of those woods for years and you just blurt it out like that."

"Sorry Billy, but like everything else at the moment they just come into my head as you speak."

"No, that's OK. It's good that you're starting to remember.

"We kept being told not to go into Darkling Woods because people had disappeared from there, but that didn't bother us…well, it bothered me but as usual not you. Anyway, after a couple of visits, nothing happened to us and I wasn't worried any more so we carried on playing in the woods. We made camps and climbed trees. We jumped out of trees pretending to be paratroopers fighting the Germans and we found springy branches, then holding on to them we would leap from high up in the trees and land safely on the ground. A bit like bungee jumping that they do now-a-days.

"We had great fun and were very happy but wouldn't have been if we knew then that back home dad had been killed not long after we were evacuated."

"Where was he killed?"

"During one of the first bombing raids on London he was working a night shift at the docks."

"Of course, his would have been a reserved occupation."

"Yes, but that didn't mean he had a cushy number. Those blokes had to work really hard on long tiring shifts. Anyway mum told me later that she did not want them to tell us because it might unsettle us. I didn't learn about it until after that night."

"That night being the night you say I disappeared."

"Yes."

"So tell me about that night, Billy."

"Charlie, I remember that night like it was yesterday. Saturday 14th August, 1943 was such a lovely evening so we decided to go up the woods. When we had been playing up there before, we saw an RAF place. You said it was empty so we ought to try to get in and see if we could find any stuff to collect. I was not at all happy about going anywhere near the place but as usual you led and I followed. We managed to crawl under the wire and there was an old Nissen hut which we got into. Well, it was a real disappointment because we searched about but there wasn't anything in it. It was completely empty.

"As we wandered about inside we saw an old cover, like a big sheet of tarpaulin stuff, and you thought it might be covering something interesting so you squeezed behind it. All went quiet and after what seemed like an age I, being the wimp that I was, started to get worried and began calling out but you didn't reply. I very gingerly crept behind the sheet and out the other side but you weren't there so now I was frightened, and then you scared the shit out of me when you suddenly grabbed hold of me. You kept on about something that I should go with you and see. But there was no way Scaredy Cat me was going to do that so you grabbed me and pulled. Then it happened."

"The explosion?"

"Yes, it was massive and ripped you away from me. I didn't receive any injuries at all but you, you were gone.

"I was hysterical, I just ran outside screaming and after a bit the RAF policeman came and grabbed hold of me but I just kept on screaming. Later an Army Officer arrived and he was very nice but I think he must have slipped me a Mickey Finn because I crashed out and slept for God knows how long.

"Eventually I was sent back to Mum but the loss of Dad and you really hit her hard, she was never the same again. This is where things got a bit weird."

"How do you mean?" Charlie asked.

"Well, first we were given a council house near Auntie Connie here on Sheppey. This here is the actual house, Charlie. I bought the place off the council in 1982."

"Did Mum apply to move here?"

"No, that was the strange thing about it."

"And Auntie Connie hadn't made arrangements for you both to move here?" An image was now coming into his head of an elderly lady who looked similar to the images of the person who was their mother.

"No, as I said, it just seemed to happen."

"Somebody must have organised it."

"Well yes, but we never found out who?"

"So what else happened?"

"When we moved to the Isle of Sheppey the war was still going on, so certain restrictions still applied. Somehow though, we always seemed to have the necessities needed to make us comfortable. It was odd and it caused friction between mum and Auntie Connie." Billy seemed slightly puffed as he continued. "When I was fifteen a letter informed me that a Shipwright Apprenticeship had been arranged for me in Sheerness Dockyard."

"Arranged for you? Didn't you know about it?"

"No, and mum didn't either. Another thing was when my time for National Service came I was excused, apparently I had a heart condition. That allowed me to continue with the apprenticeship while many others lost theirs because of the call up. Through hard times here on the Island something always turned up to help us get by. I don't know, Charlie, perhaps it's all in my mind." He paused to think. "Quite honestly, Charlie, whenever I stopped to look back on things I always felt that my life was being controlled. On the one occasion I actually spoke to someone about the feeling it was with Auntie Connie. She just put it down to the loss of you.

'You are being guided through life by Charlie now,' she said. 'He is your Guardian Angel.'

"People still continued to tell me that you had been abducted and killed although it always struck me that no-one ever spoke of a body or a burial. Anyway it didn't matter because I knew you weren't dead. We were twins and there was a bond, a connection between us that people could not and did not understand. The only people who could fully understand my frustration were other sets of twins. I knew you were alive because I could feel you.

"What I needed to do was get a message to you, to find you, wherever you were. But how?"

"So where did the Memorial idea come from?"

"That was Auntie Connie. Just after the war she became more and more concerned about the deterioration in mum's health. She wondered whether it wasn't only the loss of dad and you but also the fact that mum had moved away from her safe haven, her home. Too much had happened to her at once. Auntie suggested a Memorial Notice in the local newspaper for dad which might, in some way, have the effect of bringing him to the island and give a sense of closeness. The idea seemed to cheer mum slightly and she agreed. I immediately asked if I could place one for you. That September two notices appeared in the local newspaper.

"One for dad:

In Memory of
George Hall
A loving husband and father
Died September 1940
'We now feel you are closer to us'
Olive and Billy

"Also one from me, for you:

In Memory of
Wartime Evacuee
Charles (Charlie) Hall
Killed August 1943
Aged Ten Years
'Always remembered'
Billy.

"Of course I knew that you would only be able to read the Memoriam if you were living on the Island but a feeling that I couldn't explain told me to continue placing that notice every year. I just knew that eventually you would read or hear about it and I could wait, no matter how long it took. Yes, it was a gamble because you could have been anywhere but it worked, it took a bloody long time but it worked. My only sadness now is that mum is not here."

"Yes," Charlie paused. "When did she pass away, Billy?"

"Although she had seemed so well for a few years her health once again started to deteriorate and pneumonia took her in 1970." Again he sounded breathless as he added "I took her ashes to be placed beside dad, I took her home."

"And how about you, Billy, you seem very breathless."

"The so called heart condition which got me out of National Service never bothered me until I had a minor heart attack. I got over that all right but in my early fifties I suffered a second one, far more serious than the first. Although I could have done without the heart attack, good fortune once again came my way when I was granted a large redundancy and full pension package.

"I must say that I have had a peaceful and most enjoyable retirement but over the last couple of years the old ticker has got bad."

Billy Hall took a couple of bottles from the sideboard and emptied two tablets into the palm of his hand; he downed them with the last sip of tea in his mug.

"Are you all right, Billy?"

"Yes, the chest's just feeling a bit tight at the moment. All the excitement I think."

"You just take it easy for a while. Shall I make a fresh brew?"

"Thanks, Charlie."

While he stood making the tea in the little kitchen of Billy Hall's house, so much more now came back to him. He knew that he had to be Charlie Hall.

"Better now?" he asked as he put the mugs down.

"Yes, thank you, Charlie."

"Sure?"

Billy nodded.

"I'm glad you're here, Charlie. I was really worried in case something happened to me before I got to find you and would never see you again." He paused while he drank some of the tea. "Lovely, Charlie, you make a good cuppa." and drank down more. "What about you Charlie, do you keep well?"

"Yes, it looks like I've been lucky."

"So, are you going to tell me what you've been up to, then?"

"Well, where do I start? It has to be the explosion. For me the explosion happened in 1967, in a small village in Derbyshire and, until I spoke to you my life started on that day.

"I don't remember the explosion itself, I was only informed about it afterwards. According to what I have always been told the explosion was the result of a major gas leak in the row of houses where I lived. The houses were totally destroyed and so too, sadly, were the people living in them at the time. There were three people in one house, the Easterbrook's and their young son, Phillip. When I was found the authorities took me to be him. Because I could remember absolutely nothing prior to regaining consciousness, I knew no different. It seems Phillip was ten years old and, whether it was poor forensic work or simply because I fitted the bill, I became Phillip, the orphaned son of Ron and Jean Easterbrook.

"All I can remember of those early years were the operations and the pain. The doctors and surgeons did a wonderfully skilled job on me because apparently my head was in a hell of a mess and as you can see." He pointed in the general direction of his face and head. "No scars or joins.

"So, body healed but brain did not. Well actually there wasn't any serious damage to my brain but my memory had been completely wiped clean; I could not remember and did not know a single thing. The nurses used to tease me and say I was a ten year old baby.

"While I was there, the hospital received a visit from quite a famous American doctor who specialised in mental illness. Not that I was mentally ill but obviously did have problems and this doctor, Doctor Randolph Florrello became very interested in my case. It is to this man that I owe much for what turned out to be my future life. I have done very well, Billy, for someone who was just a mischievous lad from Bethnal Green. I don't know what the explosion did to my brain but learning and education came easy to me, so much different from what I can now remember of that dingy old school we used to attend. I went to University, Billy, would you have ever thought that possible?

"After university I teamed up again with Randolph and we worked together writing about his work with mental illness."

"Did you write about you?"

"Strangely enough, no we didn't."

"In the early 1980s Randolph started to develop Parkinson's disease and desperately wanted to return to America. Finally in 1986 he did and I went with him. We spent several years working together before he sadly died. After that I came back to England and found a little place here on the Island. Later the local newspaper offered me a job and during that time I noticed a memoriam in the Obituaries column. And the rest, as they say Billy, is history."

"You've done well, Charlie."

"That's as maybe, Billy, but do you know what? After all that has happened here this afternoon and knowing now who I am and finding out where I belonged, it all fades into insignificance. It is you who has done so well."

They both sat in silence and almost in unison, lifted their mugs to drink more of their tea.

"The thing that I don't understand, Charlie, is why you disappeared after an explosion in an old hut in 1943 Wiltshire but according to you, you survived an explosion at a house in 1967 Derbyshire."

"No, it's been puzzling me too, Billy, and as crazy as it seems, especially coming from a supposedly well-educated man with a logical mind; there is only one theory that keeps going through my head. And it would also explain why we appear different age wise."

13

At The Watermill Rest Home Ernie Whittall hesitated, not quite sure how Jack was going to take this part of his story.

"As I spoke to Billy there was only one theory going through my mind." He paused, looking at Jack. "Could the explosion have, somehow, thrown me through time?"

"Oh for God's sake, Ernie, you are not going to try to tell me you are a time traveller?"

"In the sense of an adventurer, swashbuckling through space and time; no, Jack, I am not a time traveller, but yes, I am telling you that I have travelled through time."

Jack raised his arms, as if in surrender. "All right, I have to admit that up to this point you were really starting to pull me in." He lowered his arms. "But time travel, no I don't think so Ernie, that's for books and films."

"Is it, Jack? Remember I told you that this story would sound unbelievable and totally impossible, now's the time to start thinking about the things we spoke of earlier. How could I have known those things you asked me about? I told you they were not predictions and when I said that they were things I remembered you correctly informed me that they could not be memories when they all happened long after I wrote my stories. Of course, they would be memories if I had been there." He stopped when he saw the blank expression on Jack Duggan's face. "Come on, Jack, think about it. Surely it must all be starting to fall into place now."

Ernie started to continue with his story but Jack stopped him.

"Wait a minute, Ernie, just give me a moment." After a long pause, he continued. "You are trying to tell me that originally you, Ernest William Whittall, were Charlie Hall who travelled through time to become Phillip Easterbrook."

"In a way, yes, but it was an accident. What happened was not done purposely."

"OK, okay, so whatever happened or however it happened means that you, Charlie Hall, lived as Phillip Easterbrook from 1967. During which time you stayed on the Isle of Sheppey and you lived through the events which you had previously managed to write about between 1947 and 1952, as E W Whittall."

"I did not live through all the events, Jack, quite a few of them I read and learnt about during the period that I did live there."

"All right, but when do you, and I say you as in you now, that is Ernest William Whittall. When do you come into the picture because I'm still struggling to grasp any of what you are telling me?"

"You will just have to wait a moment longer for the answer to that, because things are going to get even more complicated."

Ernie waited until he had Jack Duggan's full attention and then continued.

"I told you that I have travelled through time. Actually, Jack, I have travelled twice. The first time being in 1943 and I now know that to be exactly what happened.

"The second time I also know happened because this time I lived through it, well almost all of it. There is one slight gap which unfortunately covers the exact moment of travel but I'll explain that.

"The rest of that afternoon with Billy is indescribable. I caught up with my true life and Billy told me all about our time in Bethnal Green. He created a lovely picture of our parents and our family life. We planned to do so many things now we were together again; so exciting. But what we did not know then was that all those plans would never happen.

"Billy started to look very uncomfortable and after taking more of his pills, said that the day had been the best day of his life but very tiring for him. He felt he needed to rest so we made arrangements to meet again the following day. We gave each other the biggest, loving hug I can ever remember in my life and then said our goodbyes. I felt a bit concerned about leaving Billy but he said he would be fine so I told him to stay in his chair and I would let myself out.

"Closing the front door behind me I made towards my car, but I never reached it. A voice very close behind me said quietly 'Hello Charlie, we've been looking for you for a very long time' and before I could turn to see who it was I felt a jab in the side of my neck. Then I passed out."

Part Three

The End of the Beginning

14

Ernie Whittall took a sip from the cup that held the now cold tea. Sitting in the chair was becoming very uncomfortable and his back ached. It seems that being in bed for so long was starting to take its toll. He shifted slightly in his chair then continued.

"Exactly what happened next is when the gap occurs. As I said, I clearly remember someone saying they had been looking for me, and then feeling a sharp jab on the side of my neck. But after that is a total blank until I gradually came too.

"Looking around, I appeared to be in a sort of hospital ward but it was very basic and had been fitted out with very old equipment. The door opened and a nurse entered but this nurse reminded me of when I was in hospital as a child. Her uniform consisted of a calf-length dress with short sleeves and a large collar. Over this dress she wore an apron of almost equal length and on her head, a large cap with a pleat at the back.

'Well hello Mr Whittall, I see you are awake.'

"She lifted my arm and started to read my pulse using the little watch pinned to the bib of her apron.

'But I am not Mr Whittall,' I started to protest.

'Now you just lay quietly and I'll tell them you are awake.' She laid my arm gently back on the bed and left the room.

"A smart, well-spoken man entered next.

'Hello, Mr Hall, how are you feeling?'

'Very groggy and totally confused would be a pretty good description.'

'Yes well, the grogginess will soon wear off. As for the confusion, I suppose that is understandable.'

I tried to sit up in the bed but could not.

'Do not try to move, it will take a bit longer for the drug to clear your system. Lay and rest for the moment.'

'Drug, what drug?'

'You will be fine, don't worry.'

'Are you a doctor?'

'No. I am, well actually I'm nobody. I'm a complete unknown to everyone.'

'What?'

'In other words, Mr Hall, you do not need to know who I am.'

'Why did the nurse call me Mr Whittall?'

'Ah yes. But first I have some papers for you to sign.'

'What papers? And who do I sign them as; Charles Hall, Phillip Easterbrook or Mr Whittall?'

'Very good, I'm glad to see you have a sense of humour.'

'He opened an old briefcase and took out some papers.

'You will sign them as Ernest William Whittall.'

'Why?'

'Because, from now on that is who you are.'

'Why do I need to be someone else?'

'When you have signed these, I will tell you.'

"Although still immobile I did just manage to move my arm and hand enough to make some semblance of a signature on the first of his papers which, by the way were headed 'Official Secrets Act'. He pulled up a chair.

"Although he gave away very little information at all it was just enough to confirm that as Charlie Hall I had inadvertently travelled forward in time. Whoever he represented did not have any part in my life as Phillip Easterbrook but they needed to bring Charlie back, and now here I was; in 1946.

"They had set up a new identity for me as Ernest William Whittall and I was to make my home in a little place called Mill Edge."

"Mill Edge, where on earth is that?" Jack asked.

"Unlike its name suggests Mill Edge was not near a mill. It was in fact a tiny village consisting of a few farm houses dotted about beside Ennerdale Water. Things were not so bad because one of the houses doubled up as a pub. Mill Edge doesn't exist now but it was in the, then, county of Cumberland."

"That's the Lake District, isn't it?"

"It wasn't called that then, but yes and most of that area is now the modern county of Cumbria. They couldn't have sent me much further North without exiling me in Scotland. So, anyway, I would be given a house and an allowance to live on. I could sign the other paper he had and settle down to a life in Cumberland or," Ernie Whittall started to tremble. "It still makes me shudder when I think of the alternative to behaving."

"Murder?" Jack cut in again.

"No. Worse."

Ernie had to stop for a moment. He picked up the cup again and looked in at the cold tea; his hands were still shaking as he put it back onto the table.

"Remembering that whatever drugs they had given me were still making it virtually impossible for me to move, Mr Nobody slowly moved from the chair and sat on the side of my bed. He laid a hand on my neck.

'I will just apply a little pressure here on your Carotid Artery and before I leave the ward you will have become a dribbling vegetable for the rest of your life, never leaving this room again. Do I make myself clear?' and he gently squeezed my neck for a moment. It's amazing what fear does to you and once again I managed enough movement in my arm to scribble a signature on the other piece of paper, which was basically a contract. My agreement to behave, you might say!

'Thank you Mr Whittall, everything will be arranged.'

"He put all the papers back in his brief case then stood up from my bed and carried the chair back to the side of ward. As he moved towards the door, he turned.

'Oh, Mr Whittall,' he deliberately paused to make sure he had my attention. 'Never forget that you will be watched very carefully. If you break our contract, the consequences will be extremely dire.'

"The smile he gave as he left the room was very disturbing. I still shudder, even now, when I think of it."

The adrenalin rush that he had experienced since Jack Duggan's appearance was waning quickly and suddenly Ernie felt very tired. He tried to focus his mind; not much left to tell now.

"So, here I was now living in 1946. Okay, it wasn't so bad; I was very comfortable and did not have any more visits like that day in hospital but for me there was one big frustration. I was sitting on a treasure chest that I could not open, a treasure chest that I dare not open. I had travelled through time, both ways. Not only did I know the future and could have made myself a fortune but also had the scoop of the century for a journalist.

"It's funny how fear slowly subsides and eventually the writer and journalist in me started to take over. I needed to tell this story without putting myself in danger but I had absolutely no idea how to do it. Obviously I would never be able to write anything myself but could I find a way to tell somebody else? Could I make someone believe?

"Sending messages to the future came about by sheer accident. I had settled down and decided to resume writing, although nothing heavy like the medical works done with Randolph. An idea for children's stories had been developing in my mind because in those days there was the wireless but no television, video tapes or DVD's. No records, cassettes or CD's and no computerised games; children read books. So The Island Gang was formed.

"About this time I had a visit from Mr Nobody, obviously I had behaved myself to his satisfaction because he was quite amiable, almost friendly. I explained my idea to write children's books and he seemed to find that acceptable. I was to send the completed manuscript to a pre-arranged publisher who would check the story and, if viable, publish it. I thought to myself; for checked, read scrutinised and censored.

"In 1947, The Island Gang was released and although one hopes for success I was surprised how quickly my book became popular. The publishers wanted a second story. They had sent me a copy of the book and I felt quite proud, I couldn't stop reading it. But during the third time of indulging myself I noticed I had made a mistake. That mistake was the four concrete pillars. I hadn't noticed my error, but more to the point; neither had anyone else. An idea pushed itself forward.

"In book two, Smugglers Abound, the opening chapter was as you noticed a variation of the opening chapter of book one. Indeed, I had decided that it would be the theme through all of my stories. The concrete pillars would remain in each book. I felt that if they were spotted I could confidently explain that it was the only bridge I knew and get away with it as 'a slip of the tongue', or rather 'slip of the pen'. I also hoped they would accept the word 'cool' as a common expression that spontaneously came to mind without thinking of it as pertaining to a certain era.

"I really should have left it there but I wanted to test the water further by trying something obscure, so Sam Dixon's boat became the Ferrio Lau. I only mentioned it once but I did sweat for a long, long while after I sent that second book to the publisher. If these people had decoded the messages in the future, it would have been rather difficult to explain away. In the end my worries were unfounded because Smugglers Abound was published and, until you, nothing has ever been said.

"In book three, A Spy in the Camp, using Warners was a bit obscure to anyone not knowing the Island well. I suppose I could have cited artistic licence for a big holiday camp on the Island. And later, well it was just coincidence that they had built one there, wasn't it?

"By book four, A Ghost on the Track, I started to suspect that the stories were not being scrutinised too thoroughly and perhaps not even at all. I don't think any of those people, whoever they were, knew where the Isle of Sheppey was let alone anything about it. Even so I don't think I pushed my luck too far with the closing of the railway, although as I said to you earlier I had got dates muddled a bit. I suppose, a bit like Warner's, if anyone had been a bit sharp and noticed once again that something had happened after I had written about it; suspicions could have been aroused. But book four passed safely into children's literacy circles.

"Things were going well although there was still that underlying fear that kept me from becoming too overconfident. So in book five, Treasure in the Grounds, the reference to Screaming Lord Sutch was safe, at least until the 1960's, and The Monster Raving Looney Party until the 1980's.

"By this time I was really enjoying the subterfuge but did feel that I was pushing my luck, so decided to safeguard myself by making book six the last. The Final Chase was released in 1952 and included my references to the three prisons as well as Butlins.

"After that I sat back and enjoyed life in one of the most beautiful parts of England, just awaiting the right visitor... You took your time Jack Duggan."

At last Jack was starting to feel that this old man's story had an element of believability. "Were you ever tempted to visit Sheppey? Because you could have met up with Billy a lot earlier than you actually did and not only that, you could have met your mother."

"Oh yes, it definitely crossed my mind. But remember, Jack, I had previously lived until 1993 and had read books and articles about time travel. I had watched the films and although they were all make believe they did throw up many plausible consequences of altering events in time and bumping into one's self. Also, memories of the warning that I would be watched very carefully meant that, yes I thought about it many times but did not."

"And you continued the Memoriam?"

"By the 1990's, as Ernest Whittall, my health started to deteriorate badly and I moved into here. Of course, I knew everything that happened up to 1993, before I travelled back to 1946, but I did not know what happened beyond then. I didn't know if anyone eventually picked up on my clues and I did not know what happened to Billy. So during September of 1994 I sent for each week's edition of your newspaper and none of them had Charlie's Memoriam in the Obituaries. Sadly, from this I figured that Billy must have passed away." Jack refrained from telling him Billy had died on the same evening that Phillip Easterbrook disappeared. "I decided to continue the Memoriam from the next year and for as long as I was alive, it would now be my memorial to Billy. Also crossing my mind was the fact that if I now signed it 'Always remembered, Ernie', someone might notice and wonder why the name had changed." He looked across at Jack and smiled.

"It was actually the Memoriam that kicked things off in my mind," Jack admitted. "And when I discovered who you were, in the sense of E W Whittall; The Island Gang connection was a bit of a gamble on my part."

"I said you must be devilishly good but I am disappointed that you did not discover the clues in my books."

"Yes, I'm sorry about that Ernie. Maybe the reason was simply because although it was extremely clever to use children's books to reduce the chances of certain adults noticing what you were doing it also reduced the chances of anyone noticing."

"How do you mean?"

"Well, from personal experience as a child and I would think it the same for all children, I used to get totally engrossed in a book. I accepted everything within the story without stopping to analyse what was actually fact or fiction."

"You could be right, Jack. Anyway, now you have your scoop so it is up to you what happens next. As for me, I have not been well for a long time but was determined to hang on long enough for you to come. I honestly think that pure willpower must have pulled me through these last couple of days so that I could finally tell my story." He relaxed back into his chair. "Now my job is done; they can no longer touch me." He paused before adding almost as a last breath. "Good luck Jack Duggan and thank you."

Ernest William Whittall closed his eyes.

15

In Addlesdale the taxi picked Jack up at The Red Lion. On the journey to the station so many worrying things were going through his mind.

'If they let you tell it', Ernie had said. They did not let him, because he was abducted at the very moment he left Billy Hall. They knew he was there. Do they now know I am here? He sat quietly thinking to himself. But I have left Ernie, been back to The Red Lion to collect my belongings and am now on my way to the station, all without incident. Even so his mind would still not relax. He had to have a backup plan.

"Sorry, driver, would you just pull over to that shop. I want to buy some lunch for my journey."

He returned to the taxi carrying a carrier bag containing a large ham and cheese baguette, a doughnut and a bottle of still water.

Almost immediately after Jack Duggan's taxi had pulled away from the small shop a man entered and introduced himself as a Government Investigator. He quickly flashed a small identity card in front of the young girl at the till.

"The man that has just left, what did he do whilst he was in here?"

"He just bought a baguette, a doughnut and a bottle of water."

"It seemed to take him a long time to purchase those few items."

"Perhaps it took him a while to make up his mind about which type of baguette he fancied." And the girl smiled but the man's face remained serious.

"He bought a Jiffy bag and posted a package." The Post Office Clerk called out to him from behind her counter. He walked over to her.

"Can I see it please?"

"Oh no, I can't do that."

"I'm afraid," he said as he looked at the badge pinned to her dress. "Mrs Harrison, that my authority far outweighs any rules or regulations of The Post Office. You are obliged to co-operate with me. I will not remove the package from these premises and I guarantee there will be no problems for you - unless, of course, you refuse my request."

She passed over Jack's parcel.

Once he had taken the package from Mrs Harrison, the Investigator examined it then removed a small bag from his briefcase. Using a scalpel type instrument and liquid from a tube he carefully peeled open the seal of the envelope and looked inside. After resealing the package he next took out a device which when turned on the ladies could hear a low humming noise. First the top and bottom of the package were scanned then he ran the device around the sides. The machine and small bag went back into his briefcase and the package was returned to the Post Office Clerk as promised.

"I have to inform you, ladies, that what the man did in your shop and subsequently what I did are covered by the Official Secrets Act. You must never talk to anyone about what happened here. Do you both understand?"

"Yes."

"Yes."

"I also have to inform you that penalties for offences under National Law are far more severe than Criminal Law. Do you both understand that as well?"

"Yes."

"Yes."

"Thank you, ladies; you will not be troubled again." And the mysterious man left their shop.

A woman wearing her nurses uniform, with a badge that read 'Mrs Armstrong, Matron' sat in the driver's seat of a car parked outside. The moment he climbed into it, the car sped away.

Six people witnessed the collapse of a man, stood with a nurse and a second man, near the entrance to the station. One person offered to help but was reassured by the nurse, and the man who said he was a doctor, that everything was under control. The two medics managed to get the unconscious man into an awaiting car.

"Poor man, I hope he will be all right." A very concerned old lady's eyes followed the car as it left the scene.

Another onlooker tried to reassure her. "I'm sure he'll be fine; they'll be taking him straight to hospital."

"Yes." said a third. "He was so lucky that they arrived just as he became ill."

The group remembered the incident all day and felt excited as they spoke about it to whoever they met.

All Jack Duggan felt was a sharp jab in his neck.

The receptionist who answered Sylvia's telephone call to The Watermill Rest Home was unable to help.

"I'm sorry, Miss Stevens, we haven't seen Mr Duggan since Ernest died."

"Died, what happened?"

"Ernest had been very ill for a long time. To be truthful we expected him to pass away long ago but it almost seemed as if he were hanging on for someone. When Mr Duggan came here our Ernest came alive, as if at long last this was the person he had been waiting for. After Mr Duggan's second visit, Ernest just closed his eyes and went to sleep."

"And Mr Duggan has not been back since."

"No, I'm afraid not."

"Perhaps he is staying up there for the funeral?" Sylvia said but already doubts were starting to creep in.

"It's not until next week but if I see Mr Duggan, Miss Stevens, I will certainly tell him you telephoned."

Sylvia hoped she would hear before that so when she received the package Sylvia felt a glimmer of hope. Inside were Jack's recorder and four tapes but when she played the tapes they were all blank. She even tried them in another machine just in case the recorder had been damaged in the post, still they were blank. She also double checked the recorder itself by recording a short message, it replayed perfectly. Why had he sent her blank tapes; the glimmer of hope faded.

RAF

Westcott

16

Westcott, Wiltshire 1933.

Police Sergeant Maynard came out of his office and approached the young Constable sitting at the front desk of Westcott Police Station.

"Constable Bennison, there's a vagrant been reported loitering about on the Heath up near Darkling Woods. Get up there and send him on his way, I don't want any of them types hanging around on my patch."

"Darkling Woods, Sarge?"

"That's what I said Constable, is it a problem?"

"No, Sarge."

"Off you go then, lad."

Police Constable Colin Bennison eventually found the elderly tramp seated on a large log near the edge of Darkling Woods. Surrounded by several beer bottles, most of which were empty, his unsteady gait and slurred voice certainly showed signs that they were his bottles and he had consumed their contents.

PC Bennison quickly made it perfectly clear to the old man that his Sergeant would be down on him like a ton of bricks if he did not move on immediately and move far away. The tramp stood and wavered in front of the Police Officer. The reek of beer filled his nose as the old man spoke to him.

"Don't worry Constable we will depart of your hospitality as soon as my friend returns."

"So where has this friend of yours gone, then?" The young Police Officer asked, looking around for another person.

Wobbling, the vagrant turned to point into the woods. "Just in there."

PC Bennison took this to mean that a second tramp had possibly gone into the woods to relieve himself but as he looked through the trees the young Police Constable still couldn't see any sign of another person.

"How long has he been in there?"

"Since yesterday afternoon Constable."

He grabbed the tramps arm. "Right, come on you." and started

80

to push the old man but turned with a start when the second tramp just seemed to appear beside them. This man also seemed to be in a drunken state.

"Where were you?" the Police Constable asked, slightly alarmed.

"In there, hoccifer." The tramp slurred.

"Where?"

"In there with them."

"Who?" Bennison questioned, straining to peer through the trees.

"Them folks there."

But, as before, all that Police Constable Colin Bennison could see were trees.

Simon Eldridge was a Government scientist who had investigated many strange phenomena for a secret Government Department, a Department about which he knew very little at all. The set up was simple: he received his instructions and grants; he reported back and was paid a handsome wage in return.

For a while now he had been studying Darkling Woods. It was not the first time his attention had been directed there but previously all the strange occurrences were attributed to stories, legends and folk tales. His new brief was not only to investigate local plants and vegetation common to the area but also to trace any intoxicating fumes that might emanate from either Westcott Heath or nearby woodland. The whole purpose of the investigation was to discover if a previously unknown form of drug or gas could have caused hallucinations and contributed to the collective need to avoid Darkling Woods.

Within all the paperwork he had accumulated was a copy of the recent report made by Police Constable Colin Bennison. The Station Sergeant received an official request to allow PC Bennison leave to assist Simon Eldridge in Darkling Woods.

At the top of the Heath Officer Bennison led Simon to where the incident with the tramps had taken place.

"You can relax now Officer, you don't need to stand on ceremony with me."

"Thank you, sir."

"Colin, isn't it?"

"Yes sir."

It seemed to be as relaxed as PC Bennison was going to get.

"So, Colin, will you tell me exactly what happened and point out precisely where each moment of your encounter with the vagrants occurred."

As the Officer went through his story Simon Eldridge placed markers in the ground and made relevant notes relating to those markers and to everything Colin Bennison told him.

For the next six weeks Simon Eldridge worked in Darkling Woods. Crates full of samples were taken and then sent for analysis but each time the return reports announced that nothing from the ordinary had been found.

He began to get frustrated, which was very unusual for the scientist. Normally he was a very patient man and had the reputation of being a person who usually 'hung in there' long after others had given up, but this task was starting to get to him. No matter what he tried, he could find absolutely nothing. He hated being beaten but Darkling Woods was fighting him hard and was not going to give up its secret easily. Simon decided that he would bring in an assistant to go over all the ground he had covered just in case he had missed something. Bernard Lipscombe joined Simon in Westcott and the scientist briefed him on the investigation, going over everything that had happened and all the work he had carried out.

Simon took Bernard Lipscombe to Darkling Woods and at the spot where PC Bennison had encountered the vagrants Simon Eldridge related the story again.

"The old men were clearly drunk but the Police Officer was completely sober and states that at no time did he feel anything other than total clarity and was in full control of his senses. Basically he was trying to say that he did not feel intoxicated or drugged but he could not see the second man or where he suddenly appeared from. I have carried out tests of the area until I am sick of tests and cannot find anything that could have caused the officer to hallucinate in any way."

"Could he have been hiding in there?" Bernard Lipscombe asked.

"In where?" Simon asked trying to look beyond where the other scientist was pointing.

"Through that archway," and the assistant continued to gesture towards an area a short distance in front of them.

"An archway, you can see an archway?"

"Yes look, just over there." He moved the scientist slightly to the right then placed an outstretched arm over Simon's shoulder and pointed once again but all that Simon Eldridge could see were trees.

"Can you see it now?"

"No," Simon Eldridge stood straining his eyes in a desperate attempt to see it. "So, how big is this archway?"

"Not overly big, a bit like the entrance way through a garden wall."

Yet no matter how hard I try, Simon thought to himself. *I just cannot see it*. He called to the other scientist who had moved further into the woods. "Bernard, are you near it now?"

"Yes, I'm standing right at the entrance."

"Can you see anything inside it or through it?"

"I'll look." And he stepped forward.

"Be careful."

Bernard Lipscombe simply vanished before Simon's eyes, and then reappeared just as quickly as he had disappeared. He stood looking around at the trees with an expression of amazement on his face.

"Unbelievable."

"What?" Simon blurted out as his brain raced to analyse what his eyes had just seen.

"I saw a town," and still looking behind him Bernard added. "It was just there, where all the trees are now."

Although they were relatively confused thoughts, something exciting started to stir in Simon's mind and he started to jot down some notes:

An archway.

The tramp said there were people.

Bernard said there was a town.

It seems that only certain people can see it.

Bernard can see it and went through.

I cannot see it.

PC Bennison could not see it and probably the first tramp could not either.

The second vagrant could see it and he also went through.

It would explain all the stories of appearances and

disappearances in the legends and folk tales of mysterious happenings.

He shouted across to Bernard Lipscombe.

"This might sound silly, Bernard, but is it possible that your town was in a different time zone?"

"I don't know but it's gone now." Bernard called back.

"What, just disappeared?"

"Yes."

Another two weeks went by before Bernard could see the archway again. Now the two men had prepared a planned course of experiments for when it reappeared, they were confident that it would.

At this early point of their investigation the only certain thing they could record was that the archway came and went; how long it stayed they did not know. The first part of the experiment now was to simply wait and note how long. After twenty-two and a half hours it again disappeared. They had to wait fifteen days for the reappearance.

"Remember, Bernard, once you've entered make a note of where you are and stay there. Record everything that you see and take a few photographs but don't take any risks. Stay for no more than a quarter of an hour and then return. I'll wait here."

After exactly fifteen minutes, he returned.

"Are you okay? How did it go?"

"Yes, I'm fine and it was amazing."

"Was it the same place?"

"No, this time I went into what seemed like a park."

They packed up all their possessions and returned to the hotel so that Bernard could report fully on those fifteen minutes. If they had stayed long enough they would have noticed that the archway, or portal as they now called it, disappeared after twenty-two hours and twenty minutes.

Bernard's notes were very thorough but his photography skills were put into doubt when all of the pictures and negatives were completely blank.

"I don't know why, I know the camera worked and I was very careful with the way that I used it. Perhaps it is faulty."

Giving Bernard the benefit of the doubt Simon purchased a new camera which they tested to prove that it worked properly. On his next trip through the portal Bernard took the new camera plus, at Simon's request, he also took the photographs already produced by the new camera.

Following Bernard's return Simon was more interested in getting the camera's film developed and didn't seem as surprised as his assistant when once again the pictures and negatives were blank.

"I don't understand." A disappointed Bernard Lipscombe sighed.

"I think I do." Simon gave him a sympathetic pat on the shoulder. "Have you got the pictures you took with you?"

"Yes, here they are."

The pictures were still in the same condition as when they travelled through the portal.

"Am I missing something, Simon?"

"I think, Bernard, that we won't be able to use photography to record the future."

"Why?"

"Look at the pictures you took with you."

"There's nothing wrong with them."

"Exactly, because the events we photographed here have already happened so therefore the camera recorded them and the photographs behaved like any other photograph, allowing us to see events from the past. But the pictures of what you photographed in the future could not pass backwards in time because they have not happened yet. Technically, then, the camera hasn't taken the pictures and the film is blank."

"Confusing, but I see what you mean."

Over the next few months the two scientists continued with their tests, now relying on written reports and simple sketches. Bernard stayed for longer periods each time, noting as much information as he could while all the time making sure that he kept out of danger. Gradually they established that the portal randomly opened into five different places, five gates. So far, the gates always seemed to open into the future. Although, again, when in the future seemed to vary each time. The return journey was always to the same time and place, which was a relief to Simon because it had crossed his mind that he would not know what to do if his assistant did not come back. He had now become a very confident traveller and Bernard noted more and more information each time he went through the portal but they both agreed that they really needed to find some more travellers.

Eighteen days between appearances and twenty-one hour before its disappearance.

The time came for Simon's report and journeys through the portal were suspended.

Two men, Lieutenant General James Hempstead and Air Commodore Arthur Theobald were assigned to work alongside Simon Eldridge on the project. It was given the code name of 'Watchett' after Mrs Watchett, the housekeeper to the time traveller in H G Wells' The Time Machine. Knowledge of the project would be kept a secret from everyone, including the Military and His Majesty's Government.

There was one other person and it was he who protected and safeguarded the committee and 'Project Watchett'. But he was unknown to those three committee members and they only communicated with him through a very complicated and secret coding system.

The decision was made to hide and isolate the portal by building a small nondescript military site around it but first an idea to recruit more travellers was devised.

One thousand military personnel were given a simple observation test, which involved Bernard Lipscombe standing amongst the trees in Darkling Woods. At times arranged by Simon Eldridge the personnel, in small groups, were asked to report exactly what they saw:

- Seven hundred and sixty-two gave an almost perfect description of the man standing amongst trees.
- Two hundred and thirty-four gave a poor description of the man standing amongst trees.
- Four gave a good description of the man standing at the entrance to an archway in amongst the trees.

After thorough and extensive checks on service records, personalities and reliability of the four who had seen the portal only three were felt to be suitable. Ultimately two males and one female joined Bernard Lipscombe as travellers.

Journeys into the future resumed and as the travellers became more skilled they stayed for longer periods each time.

While the project recorded more and more events from the future many things were very unsettling. But because they had no control over the portal and were extremely amateurish at time travel, they had no idea of the consequences of what they were doing. So there had to be one major rule: *Under no circumstances must any alteration to events be carried out, no matter how harrowing that event may be.*

As the 1930s progressed an event loomed even nearer, an event and it's horrors that Project Watchett was aware of but could not change. It was imperative that they stuck by their rule. Their one consolation being that they knew the outcome.

With the war fast approaching all work on Project Watchett halted but not entirely due to the war. Other things happened including the disappearance of three of the five original gates. The portal was now up to three months between appearances and only remained open for three and a half hours and Simon feared that it was, slowly closing itself down. Also one traveller, Naval Petty Officer Alan Bane, had failed to return. The mystery of what happened to him was finally solved when RAF Westcott received a visit on the 9th April, 1938.

It was Lieutenant General James Hempstead who picked up the receiver of the telephone.

"Hempstead."

"Guardroom, Sir. I have a Mr Emmerson here. He is a solicitor with Emmerson and Emmerson, solicitors, in the village. He has a letter for you."

"A solicitor delivering letters"

"Yes Sir."

"Ask him to leave it with you and I will collect it later."

"Sorry, Sir, but he says he must hand it to you personally. He's pretty insistent, Sir."

"Put him on the line."

After a short pause another voice came over the telephone. "Good morning, Lieutenant General."

"Good morning, Mr Emmerson. I understand that you have a letter for me but you cannot leave it at the gate."

"That is correct."

"Can you tell me why?"

"I could give you a very brief outline as to why not, but the purpose of my visit must be completed with you in person."

"Not something you can just tell me over the telephone?"

"I'm sorry, but no."

"Very well, I will be out shortly," and James Hempstead put down the receiver.

If you were to be asked what he did for a living you would almost certainly say 'Solicitor'. There was just something about Peter Emmerson that gave the impression and, of course, his pinstriped suit stood out amongst the everyday wear of others in the small village of Westcott. The grip was rather limp and loose as he shook hands with Lieutenant General Hempstead.

"So, Mr Emmerson, fire away."

"In April of 1912 my father, George Emmerson, took receipt of a letter." he raised an envelope. "The explicit instruction was that it must not be opened and that it must be handed to Lieutenant General James Hempstead at RAF Westcott on 9th April 1935. It was very strange because at the time there was no RAF or RAF Westcott. We have always wondered…"

"1935, you said 9th April 1935?"

"Yeesss, from what I understand, the letter was passed to a Clerk to log in the firm's records and then be put into storage. But it appears that the Clerk's writing was misread and 1935 read as 1938. So I must profoundly apologise and sincerely hope that no damage has been caused by the delay."

"Well let's see, shall we."

The solicitor passed over the envelope and the Lieutenant General examined it. James Hempstead looked towards the Solicitor. "I can confirm that the envelope is still sealed and intact, if that's what you needed me to do," then he carefully opened it. He removed the letter, written in the form of a telegram and read: *Westcott 8th April 1912. Went backwards stop Gate closed stop Travelling to Southampton stop Hoping to board Titanic stop Finale for a hopelessly marooned naval man stop Bane*

17

The Final Meeting of Project Watchett, 1947.

The first words of dismay came from Air Commodore Arthur Theobald.

"I really thought this whole issue had finally been resolved."

"And so did I," Simon Eldridge scowled. "It should never have taken so long to realise what Ernest Whittall had done in his books."

The Air Commodore looked at Lieutenant General James Hempstead. They had hoped to avoid talking about this part in the issue.

"You're right, Simon." James Hempstead sounded slightly uneasy. "But it was very clever to use children's books and a location we knew virtually nothing about. They were just seen as innocent adventure stories and no one took them seriously."

"And when the discrepancies were discovered?"

"It was too late to do anything about it."

"So, the whole blunder was ignored?"

"Indeed not, Simon." The Lieutenant General answered positively. "Things were made a little easier for us because the health of Whittall was failing and he had been in a rest home for some while. A traveller was put in place to keep a close eye on him and until Jack Duggan there were no causes for concern."

"How do we know that someone hasn't discovered Whittall's deception beforehand?" The scientist once again made the other two men feel uncomfortable.

"Well, we don't but there have never been any blips or unusual occurrences to suggest that anyone has."

"It seems, then, that Mr Duggan was the only person over the decades to cotton on to what was in the books."

"Yes, Simon, and we were there when he came on the scene." James Hempstead felt that he had swayed the conversation back his way.

"We were lucky, gentlemen, that nothing happened prior to Mr Duggan."

"Yes, and we were all prepared when it did happen." The Lieutenant General felt rather smug until Simon Eldridge's response brought the three men back to the reason for their meeting.

"But something still went wrong?"

The silence between the three men lasted for several minutes as they each tried to focus their thoughts on to what had actually happened during Jack Duggan's abduction.

"Are we absolutely sure he did not arrive back here? Perhaps he gave us the slip, Simon." It was Lieutenant General James Hempstead who spoke first. Before Simon could speak the Air Commodore asked.

"Was Jack Duggan able to travel?"

"Yes." Simon answered.

"Did we know that?"

"No."

"It sounds to me as if the whole exercise was very risky."

"There was a backup option." Lieutenant General Hempstead gave the Air Commodore a knowing look as he spoke.

"What? Oh, right." Suddenly realising what the Lieutenant General meant, he asked. "Are you sure that option wasn't taken?"

"Yes." Simon continued. "He definitely travelled because our team sent him first and followed once they knew he could travel; they arrived but he did not. Also, Mr Duggan was unconscious so he couldn't have done anything by himself."

"Are you suggesting that he had help?" The Lieutenant General was quick to respond and the scientist was equally as quick to answer.

"No, no James I am just saying that he could not have done anything because he was unconscious. I wasn't implying that someone else did."

"Okay," Air Commodore Theobald stepped in. "We do not appear to be getting anywhere here." He turned towards the Scientist. "Do you have any theories at all, Simon?"

"I do, but I have to cover the whole rather than just Jack Duggan." He looked towards the two other men in case there was any sign of protest. When there wasn't he continued. "I believe, gentlemen, I can confidently say that you think our problems started when Charlie Hall disappeared. Am I right?"

"Yes." Air Commodore Theobald responded without

hesitation.

"Well, I'm not so sure," Lieutenant General Hempstead expressed doubts. "There always seemed to be problems cropping up." The Air Commodore gave him a strange look.

"Exactly," Simon replied. "I think the whole project has been a problem. Yes it did complicate things when the boy disappeared but the problems began right from the very start.

"We could never control the portal and never knew where the travellers would go or to which time zone. The only thing we knew, or thought we knew, was that they went to the future and always came back here."

The other men nodded in agreement.

"The next part of my theory is going to be difficult to understand but I think that far from controlling, or rather trying to control the portal, it controlled us."

"Ridiculous." Air Commodore Theobald blustered. "You are saying an inanimate object can plan and carry out things rationally. Ridiculous."

"Ridiculous, Arthur?, Don't you think it was strange that we could never pick or choose the time zone or place to which we travelled but then suddenly we were able to send someone directly to Ernest Whittall?"

Arthur Theobald mumbled to himself as Simon carried on speaking. "The portal was far from an inanimate object, it was an entity in its own right; a portal through time." As the Air Commodore drew a deep breath, Simon quickly added. "And no, I don't mean an entity like ghosts and spirits or even little green men and things from outer space, Arthur. But the portal was definitely an unknown force which had a defence mechanism, a form of protective intelligence." Again Arthur Theobald drew a deep breath and once again the scientist did not give him chance to speak. "Not a brain or intelligence in the sense that you are thinking." He looked at the two men. "Perhaps I should call it a system of self-preservation."

"I've never heard so much nonsense." The Air Commodore spluttered as he almost leapt from his chair.

The Lieutenant General stepped in. "Sit down Arthur, let's give Simon chance to expand on his theory." Air Commodore Theobald sat back down in his chair.

"Thank you." Simon sighed and then continued. "Almost from

the moment Bernard Lipscombe found it, the portal knew what a total 'balls up' we would make of the opportunity it had given us. From the records we kept," and he lifted up a pile of notes. "You can see that almost immediately it started to reduce the time between appearances and shorten the time it remained open. In effect, gentlemen, it started closing itself down to limit the damage we could cause.

"When Charlie vanished there was an explosion but no-one caused that explosion and no physical damage was done. What did happen though, was that other gates within the portal closed; permanently."

"I didn't know about that." The Air Commodore took the opportunity to butt in again.

"It's all in the reports, Arthur." And the scientist once again lifted the paperwork. "The explosion was our second warning."

"Second?" This time it was Lieutenant General Hempstead.

"The first was sending Alan Bane into the past and then closing down the gate preventing him from ever returning. The portal was flexing its muscle.

"Once Charlie had been returned the portal gave us our last warning, although we didn't know it yet, when it closed all means of travelling forward. It remained just long enough to allow our travellers to complete the final mission and return. Now that everything is finalised it has closed itself down completely."

"It's such a shame." Lieutenant General Hempstead felt almost sad. "It had so many possibilities."

"Possibilities yes, but far outweighed by the dangers I would say." Simon quickly responded and then added. "There are too many examples of scientific discoveries being misappropriated for power or financial gain by the few instead of benefiting the whole of mankind."

"But we kept strictly to the rule of no interference, Simon, there were no dangers here"

"Were there not?" He looked from one man to the other. "Because of a simple accident we have not only changed the lives of Charlie and Billy Hall but also, either directly or indirectly, everyone and everything around them." The scientist paused to let the point sink in. "How many accidents can there be?" Another pause, "Although we made stringent checks on our travellers what if a rogue traveller managed to pass through those checks? There is no end to the damage he or she might cause." Other thoughts crossed his mind. "And what about after us; would the right people take charge of the project? With our present situation for example, we now know what Whittall did, and more so, that he is about to start his little scheme very soon. Technically we could change things so that the issue does not arise, but because we have a duty to uphold our policy of non-interference we won't. Can we be confident that those following us will be as morally conscientious of their responsibilities?" Simon slowly shook his head. "No, gentlemen, I think the portal sensed the dangers that human kind posed. It was far too valuable, far too volatile to be entrusted to mankind."

The Air Commodore was still not convinced. "Sorry Simon, but it still sounds far-fetched to me. We are pretty sure that the portal has been behind all those legends and tales for centuries, so why did it decide to close down right now?"

"Because it had not been exploited until we came along."

"Exploited, you think we exploited the portal?" The Lieutenant General asked.

"Yes, of course we did. Up to a few years ago, apart from an occasional mishap, the portal remained undiscovered and unused. Then suddenly we went mad with our new toy."

"This is all ridiculous nonsense." The Air Commodore still huffed and puffed.

"That's as may be, but I would like to know if you have any better theories." Again he looked questioningly at both men. "What we do know is that now all the outstanding issues have been resolved it has gone. The portal is no more, Project Watchett is no more."

"But we don't know that the Jack Duggan issue is resolved." Air Commodore Theobald brought the conversation back to the main subject.

"Obviously the portal thinks that it is."

"And that's why it has completely closed down." The Air Commodore was starting to grasp Simon Eldridge's theory.

"Yes."

"Damage limitation?" The Air Commodore finally conceded.

"I suppose you could say that, yes."

After the three men had calmed down, Lieutenant General James Hempstead turned to the scientist.

"So, come on Simon, what happened to Jack Duggan?"

"I think there is one possible answer but again it is only a theory, a guess."

"Which is?" The Air Commodore asked in a calmer manner.

"Earlier I spoke of the portal giving us a warning when it sent Alan Bane into the past, rather than into the future. Also, I said 'Once Charlie had been returned the portal gave us our last warning, although we didn't know it yet'."

"You think Jack Duggan was also sent into the past?" Lieutenant General Hempstead finished Simon's theory.

"I have no other suggestions."

"How far back has he gone and where has he gone?"

Simon Eldridge shrugged his shoulders.

"Unless, like Alan Bane, he sends us a letter, gentlemen, I doubt we will ever know."

Epilogue

Quite when Michel Nostradamus first met John Dygen has never been recorded, in fact there does not appear to be any mention of the knowledgeable Englishman in any documentation of that period. The man who refused to speak of his past told no-one exactly where he came from or where he had been educated in all the things he knew. Nostradamus became enthralled by this mysterious man with his strange stories and beliefs. They soon became firm friends.

As Nostradamus travelled through France treating victims of the Plague, Dygen suggested to him that he should be trying to prevent the spread rather than attempting a cure. He spoke of practising effective cleanliness and hygiene, plenty of fresh air, of encouraging healthy diets and most importantly removing infected corpses from the streets. Using these ideas, Nostradamus's effective reduction in the number of people contracting the plague was impressive.

During the 1530s Nostradamus left France and travelled through Italy, Greece and Turkey accompanied by his friend John Dygen. Whilst on these travels their in depth discussions started to veer towards astrology and mysticism. Around this time the Englishman first confided in Nostradamus about a manuscript which predicted events that would happen in the future.

Eventually Nostradamus returned to France to resume his practices for fighting the Plague. But this time the Plague fought back when it claimed his good friend, and while John Dygen lay close to death he again spoke of the manuscript.

"Michel, it is your destiny."

During the 1540s Nostradamus gradually moved away from medicine and more towards astrology and during much of this time he concentrated on John Dygen's manuscript.

The manuscript was written in a form of English, Nostradamus had not seen before and, not having a good understanding of the English language, it took him almost a decade to translate. There were so many strange things his good friend had written about that he could not understand, but he continued to transcribe John Dygen's work. The final outcome was a manuscript recorded in

Nostradamus's hand but was a combination of what Dygen had written and Nostradamus's deciphering of the strange English language. There were many parts of the manuscript where he had to make guesses as to the meaning of what his friend had written. Many of his inaccuracies during the translation process would later cause confusion to scholars of Nostradamus's work. But in 1555 the task was completed.

Michel Nostradamus published Les Prophesies, the collection of long term predictions for which he is most famous today. The Prophesies have caused many arguments over the years because they are always dependent on how each individual interprets them. The main reason for this is because, possibly fearing religious persecution, Nostradamus had devised a method of obscuring John Dygen's predictions. He used a combination of quatrains (four lined verses) and word games plus a mixture of various languages. What happened to the original work John Dygen had given to his friend will never be known but it is almost certain that Nostradamus destroyed it.

John Dygen's manuscript had foretold of events throughout the following four hundred and fifty years but did not continue beyond the end of the twentieth century. Nostradamus took this as a sign that the world would come to an end around the year 2000.

Foot Note.

Sylvia Stevens retired in 2004 and moved to Addlesdale in Yorkshire. Remembering the few things that Jack had asked or spoken about she hoped to discover what happened in 1999.

Air Commodore Arthur Theobald and Lieutenant General James Hempstead both had long and distinguished service careers.

Simon Eldridge continued to work for the Government during World War Two. In 1948 he started teaching science and went on to be a University lecturer.

Mr Nobody – It's of no surprise to say that 'nobody knows'.

Bernard Lipscombe worked alongside Simon Eldridge until the end of the war. In early 1946 he had started to develop mental problems and began to talk openly about Project Watchett. On the 14th June 1946 his body was found in a small flat in London. No autopsy or investigation was ever carried out. Official paperwork recorded 'Suicide due to mental instability'.

Immediately after Project Watchett the remaining male traveller and the female traveller disappeared. Nothing about them is known.

Alan Bane: Within all the documentation regarding the ill-fated RMS Titanic there is no record of an Alan Bane either perishing or surviving on that tragic night.

Dans le septième mois de Rome,
Une mille se tient avant le vingt sept divisé de manière égale,
un lion sera projetée en arrière
et le renard ruse de Στέφανος elle entendra rien de plus et affliger.

Malcolm R Gibbs

Following a mixture of careers including a Chef, Aerial Installer, T.V. Engineer, Security Officer and twenty plus years in a School environment Malcolm finally retired in 2016. Living with Jan, his partner of fifteen years, on the Isle of Sheppey each day is taken up fully. Interests include Family History, an Allotment and Tai Chi. He is a volunteer at Bluetown Heritage Centre where he is involved in cataloguing their artefacts and acting as a Tour Guide. Writing "The Island Gang Narratives" was part of his long term (hopefully) 'Bucket List'.

www.ingramcontent.com/pod-product-compliance
Lightning Source LLC
Chambersburg PA
CBHW070510130626
46555CB00003B/1231